grydscaen
insurrection

Natsuya Uesugi

Copyright © 2021 by Natsuya Uesugi

All rights reserved. This book or any portion thereof may not be reproduced or transmitted in any form or manner, electronic or mechanical, including photocopying, recording, or by any information storage or retrieval system, without the express written permission of the copyright owner except for the use of brief quotations in a book review or other noncommercial uses permitted by copyright law.

Printed in the United States of America

ISBN: Softcover   978-1-63871-011-0
       eBook   978-1-63871-010-3

Republished by: PageTurner Press and Media LLC
Publication Date: 05/11/2021

To order copies of this book, contact:

PageTurner Press and Media
Phone: 1-888-447-9651
order@pageturner.us
www.pageturner.us

Works by Natsuya Uesugi

SciFi Novels
grydscaen: utopia – prelude
grydscaen: beginnings – prologue
grydscaen: retribution – volume 1
grydscaen: war – volume 2
grydscaen: tribute – anthology
grydscaen: alliance – volume 3
grydscaen: insurrection – volume 4
grydscaen: dissonance – anthology

Dark Fantasy Novels
The Alchemist's Ranger - prologue
The Seer of Grace and Fire: book 1
The Seer of Ice and Sky: book 2

Cyberpunk Novellas
A Storm's Coming
Rogue
Read Only Memory
the seal maker
grydscaen: dark
grydscaen: scout

Yaoi Novellas
graphic noiz: book 1 - 6

Manga
A Storm's Coming
graphic noiz manga 1 & 2

Book Dedication

To Tsuyoshi, my friend from high school who followed his dream and became an officer and a pilot in the Air Force. The pilots in grydscaen are a testament to your courage and the drive and discipline it takes to attend the Air Force Academy. Even though I ran track meets at West Point every year with the Varsity team and won a lot of medals doing it, that discipline thing would have been my undoing.

To all those young adults who are searching, questioning or just trying to find your way, may the journey on this rainbow path be full of courage. May the stories in grydscaen provide just a little glimmer of hope. This is why I write grydscaen, so there are stories that were not available when I was 16 and trying to find my place in the world. From Faid and the Packrats, to Sati in the Pacific Territories military, you are strong and can be divine. Stay fierce my pretties!

for more on grydscaen

Visit http://natsukoarts.com

On the Cover: Sati Ima, the Quadrion Isshin mobile frame pilot and former Psi Faction test subject in his flight suit on the battleship Escalon.

Illustrations

Cover illustration by Natsuya Uesugi

Interior Illustrations: Map and Sati Ima in cockpit by Natsuya Uesugi.

Interior Illustration: Quadrion Isshin mobile frame mecha design and concept by Natsuya Uesugi.

Characters

Ameliano "Lino" Dejarre – Son of the Viceroy. Half brother to Riuho. Member of the Psi:Ko, part of the Psi Faction. Has psychic power, is a distiller. His psychic power manifests as lightening. Is a citizen. His father and mother are residents of the City. He has a little brother and little sister. Becomes the SubViceroy.

Julian "Blue" Iskafiin – Member of the Psi:Ko, part of the Psi Faction since he was five. Has psychic power. Is a damper, can absorb the power of other psychics. Transgender.

Raven Allen – Originally from the Zone, he becomes a member of the Psi:Ko when he is kidnapped with his brother by trackers. He does not have a construct, they removed it during his psi conditioning so he no longer has control over his power.

Faid Callen – Founder of the Packrats, a psychic organization of hackers. Is kidnapped by the Psi Faction and becomes a

Psi:Ko. Is also a host and a neurocyne addict. Becomes the knight to the SubViceroy.

Gailen Allred – Runs the day to day operations of the Psi Faction. Jai is the lead guard who works under Gailen.

Chris Escani – The Psi Coordinator and a scientist for the Psi Faction. In charge of mind control.

Fred Thompson – Quadrion Isshin squadron leader on the battleship Escalon.

Sati Ima – Test subject and member of the Psi:Ko. Friend to Blue. Is a damper. Has a history of schizoaffective disorder. Left the Psi Faction and joined the Air Force with Nathaneal Barjan.

Gloughster Illian – Son of the Emperor of the Pacific Territories. Becomes the official Trance Channeler to Lino when he becomes the Sub Viceroy. From the Jannassee Islands.

Saya Amalphi – Adept and friend to Gloughster, is the servant in his service. From the Jannassee Islands.

Saito Ima – Father to Sati and Supreme Commander of the Esset battlefleet.

Prologue

In the year After Colony 2055 there was the Great War. Government scientists harnessed their knowledge of nuclear weapons and created a new form of energy using their expertise in atomic fusion. This power was called kedek energy and was a natural found occurance that existed in pools far inside the planet. The scientists harnessed this energy into weapons called kedek bombs. The Atlantea Federation, a group of nation states released these new weapons on their own people and then later on the world and changed the influence of power over the continents. The Atlantea Federation took over 75% of the world's territories.

Falling under the harsh rule of the Atlantea Federation's iron fist, many areas rebelled starting with a small nation in the Pacific Ocean called the Jannassee Islands. The Jannassee Islands formed a coalition with neighboring islands and nation states, including the United Municipalities, and their coalition became known as the Pacific Territories.

In 2056 the Pacific Territories retaliated in a full scale world war that was called the Blood Red Incident. As retaliation for this attack the Atlantea Federation unleashed their ultimate weapon called the Dionysis Effect and devastated the middle regions and many continents. Many people died due to the Dionysis Effect. However those that survived in certain areas, started to show up with the ability to do supernatural things. This was the result of the aftermath of the Dionysis Effect, the radiation from the device created something called Codess, which manifested as psychic power. These powers included teleportation, telekinesis, the ability to communicate without speaking called sending, distiller - psychic influence of other people, the ability to see into the future – known as the timestream, the ability to replicate or sway through mind control, the ability to damp – consume other people's psychic power, and the ability to heal by laying on hands. In order to control this psychic power, scientists created chemical compounds called psi inducer drugs. The most potent psi inducer drug was called neurocyne and it was a class 6 narcotic. Without neurocyne psychics could lose control of their power and destroy things, which later came to be known as psi crit. A black market grew around psi inducer drugs. The government tried to clamp down by declaring the unlicensed sale of psi inducer drugs illegal.

A whole religion grew up around codess power. Codess power was said to be a gift from the goddess. The people that followed this religion and were psychic were called the Prophets. The text that outlined this gift from the goddess Llwellyn, was called the Parable of Thoth. Llwellyn was consort to the great god of wisdom Thoth, and with his dark lord brother Set, they created the world.

The Jannassee Islands which was the seat of power for the Pacific Territories started mobilizing and organizing their various nation states and territories into zones. In one area they created the City which was a bastion of culture. Near this area they also created the Echelons which was a lower economic area and adjacent to that they created the Zone. They divided up society into citizens and non citizens. Only citizens of the Pacific Territories could reside in the City. The Zone became a place of strife, poverty and devastation. The Echelons became known for illegal drugs, prostitution, the Red Light District and crime. The Elite was formed as the governmental structure of the Pacific Territories, they ruled over the City, the Echelons and the Zone with a military might. But even though they created the Zone Police to keep order, this codess power started to cause a problem.

The scientists in the Pacific Territories created organizations to help to quell this new found danger and the unrest and terrorism that ensued due to codess power. They created the SenseNet to research codess power and create drugs and a means to control it. They created the Psi Faction as a military entity to round up errant psychics and reeducate them. And they created the Corporation and the Syndicate as a multinational conglomerate to market and sell their processes and products. The Psi Faction had a clandestine force of psychic soldiers, called the Psi:Ko. However with this new found power came exploitation, the Psi Faction started rounding up people off the street and experimenting on them trying to learn more about this codess power and ways to manipulate it for defense capabilities. The Elite and the Zone Police ruled in a state of near martial law, no one was safe.

In the Echelons a group of hackers rose up to fight the manipulation and reign of terror that was being forced down on the populace by the Elite. They fought to open up society and free people from dictatorial rule. They fought through guerrilla and cyber terrorist tactics and vowed to create open source code that would free up society through information technology. They would see the Elite turned to dust. This group was called the Terror Hack and they vowed to free society from the evils of the Elite. The leader of the Terror Hack was named Mage. Seraph Gentry was one of his operatives who had been placed as a plant into the Corporation to spy on their software development and infrastructure projects.

The Psi Faction continued their experiments on errant psychics. The Zone Police learned to harness the power of subliminal messaging and they started to try to influence and control the populace through mass media taking over the airwaves, phone lines and the network with their messages.

Finally a group of renegade psychics had enough. The various groups came together in an organization known as the Packrats. Though not as militant as the Terror Hack, the goal of the Packrats was to free society and make a place safe for psychics to live away from the confines of the Elite and the Psi Faction. Their leader was a young psychic named Faid Callen and he vowed to free society through cyber revolution.

The leader of the Pacific Territories, the Emperor appointed a Viceroy over the City, the Echelons and the Zone that was responsible for ruling the people. The Viceroy's autocratic policies were harsh and devastating to people with codess power.

The Viceroy's son Ameliano Dejarre, a psychic who had the distiller power, to influence people with his will, was trained as a child to harness his codess power and was recruited to the Psi Faction. Along with his fellow psychics, the Psi Faction was tasked with destroying the Packrats and controlling the terrorist violence these errant psychics created.

The Viceroy had many consorts, one of his other sons, Riuho Dejarre had been rounded up by the Psi Faction and experimented on because he had psychic power. Riuho had been banished as a child. But one thing the Viceroy didn't know was that this experimentation and harsh treatment would change Riuho and send him down a path of retaliation and destruction.

While the Pacific Territories were dealing with its own problems of errant psychics, the Altantea Federation was trying to win back the regions that the Pacific Territories had freed. The world was divided down the middle, the Pacific Territories having rescued countless nations from the harsh rule that the Atlantea Federation was wielding. But even as the Pacific Territories tried to unite internally, the Atlantea Federation continued to be a threat to it's autonomy. The Psi Faction would soon be roped into a larger fight for the freedom of the Pacific Territories and its people.

The military created weapons called mobile frames. These weapons took on many forms. The air force and the navy used these weapons in campaigns against the Atlantea Federation. One such set of mobile frames called the Quadrion could transform from a frame configuration into a super maneuverable jet fighter. The SenseNet used their superior scientific and engineering knowledge and created mobile frames that could harness a pilot's psychic power to help to pilot the machine. These bio induced relays that were used to help inline with the machine, directly linking the brain to a bio neural net, were called jacks. A jack was installed in the brain at the temple and would allow the person with the jack to communicate with any mainframe, PC, deck or terminal through the jack inline, called a terminus cable, directly through electrical impules. Psychics got a hold of this technology and an underground market for jacks appeared in the Echelons. Hackers started getting jacks to help them hack into more sophisticated systems. They used virtual reality headgear and gloves called senso gloves to assist with these hacks. The Packrats became legendary in their use of jack technology.

As the Pacific Territories continued its fight, human beings began to evolve some with psychic powers and others with changes in physical traits. These changed humans whose skin became albino white and who grew scales and had psychic power came to be known as the Jannai. Some even had wings. The Jannai were looked down upon. In the City, being a Jannai became a crime and using codess power became a capital offense. The Atlantea Federation used these mutated humans as expendable soldiers. Through the use of drugs and mental manipulation they enslaved the Jannai and had them do their dirty work. The Jannai forces became known as killing machines due to their brutality. As time went on the Atlantea Federation substituted half of its fighting force with Jannai soldiers who were psychic.

The Atlantea Federation continued its push to regain its territory at the same time that the Psi Faction in the Pacific Territories tried to quell the destruction caused by the Packrats and the Terror Hack. The Pacific Territories were locked in a battle of wills fighting for its survival in an ever increasing violent war with the Atlantea Federation.

The 'gridscan' is what hackers called the network. An alternate spelling, 'grydscaen' was used when written in Packrat hacker code.

And so we begin...

What Has Gone Before

The Packrats attacked the Jannai Trance Channeler Isk from the Atlantea Federation and captured him, taking him to Lino, the SubViceroy. Lino's father, the Emperor now in the Jannassee Islands orders Lino to execute the prisoner as an enemy of the Pacific Territories. In a bizarre scene Isk in Jalleen's body and Lino are seen fighting at the execution and Lino captures Isk again only to take him to a cell in the palace.

Lino attacks the captured Isk and mutilates his body, only to have Isk send out his consciousness and change bodies escaping the Pacific Territories' grasp.

Chris, at the Psi Faction drugs Lino and does an experiment on him raising his psi level. Lino is livid and in a show of opposition confronts his father and orders him to treat him like a human being, stop the Psi Faction experiments on him and his team mates, nullify the marriage with Lino's 8 year old sister and free his 10 year old brother from becoming the Viceroy in Lino's stead.

A power struggle ensues at the Packrat Sprawl and Naito battles Shine in a dangerous video game that could actually end up killing the players in order to determine who will lead the Packrat Wastes. Dark takes Faid out in a mobile frame and he is wounded when the Atlantea Federation ambushes them in the Zone. Faid is hurt which causes the Packrats to be without a leader, since the Saicho cannot rule the Packrats if he is wounded. Set, Faid's mate pair, becomes the head of the Packrats for a short time until Faid recovers from his wound and then confronts Set in front of all the Packrats vying for the Saicho position back. Faid wins the fight and wounds Set in a challenge to the death. Set is fortunately healed and then Faid banishes him from the Packrats and he leaves to join the Terror Hack.

Isk, in his new body starts molesting Lino because it is Jannai mating season. Lino starts acting abusive to Gloughster keeping the molestation a secret. Finally, Lino has had enough, he attacks Isk and maims him, only to have Isk change bodies yet again and escape.

The political Elite and the Emperor convene in a meeting and agree to appoint Lino as the Viceroy. An official ceremony at the palace for Lino's coronation is interrupted by a group of Jannai who kidnap Lino, his knight and his Trance Channeler and take them to the Mendelson Space Colony where the Eleni, the codess scientists have their headquarters. The Eleni raise Lino's psychic power and then Lino returns to the planet with Gloughster and Faid, his knight.

Faid finds out that Blue manipulated him when they became mate pairs and that Blue is actually the mate pair lead due to the fact that Blue's psi level was higher than Faid's when they were paired. This puts Faid in a compromised position as the leader of the Packrats.

A map of the Eastern Region with territorial boundaries for the Atlantea Federation and the Pacific Territories

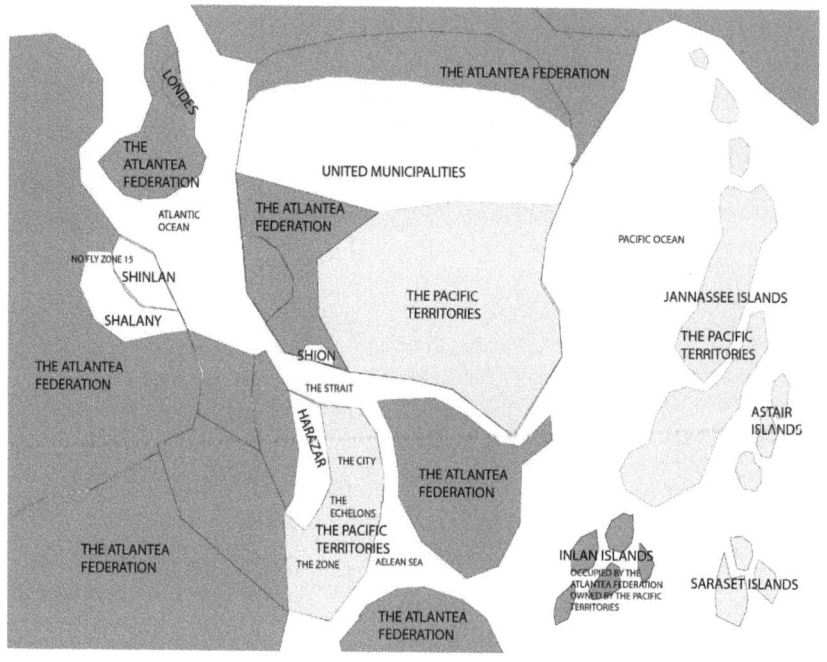

Chapter 1

"I want a jack," said Blue releasing Faid and walking to the other side of the room, taking a helmet off the shelf. He handed the helmet to Faid. He didn't know what Blue was planning.

"The Packrats will not jack you," said Faid.

"I think you will," said Blue. He took a motorcycle jacket from the rack and put it on motioning Faid to follow. "You want to be the mate pair lead. Right now I lead and this is what I want. I will tell the Packrat collective unless you do this. That would be bad for you."

Faid and Blue had still not consummated their mate pair relationship. Faid was waiting until Parat, the joining holiday. It was a few weeks till Parat. Blue walked out of the room and Faid followed. They walked to the garage at the Psi Faction. Blue put his helmet on and sat on the bike and motioned Faid to get on behind him. Blue started up the motorcycle, they would ride back to the Packrat Sprawl. Blue was manipulating Faid and Faid really had no choice in the matter, Blue was the lead. Faid got on the motorcycle behind Blue and Blue took off streaming out of the garage.

They drove through the Shizuoko ghetto recklessly. Faid had to hold on tight to make sure he didn't fall off. This was not like Blue, thought Faid. But Blue was determined. They left the motorcycle near an abandoned building and teleported into the Acolyte Forward Base. Faid pulled off the helmet and went up to Acolyte and sent to him.

You will jack him, Faid pointed to Blue as he took off the helmet.

No, I will not, he is Jannai.

I need you to do this. It is for the pair relationship, sent Faid.

Acolyte just looked at him and he knew. Blue was the lead that made him the head of the Packrats.

You didn't know this when you were paired? sent Acolyte.

I didn't think it would matter. Just jack him and then he will relinquish the pair lead to me.

Acolyte sighed they could not have a Jannai as the head of the Packrats. The technician came over to the psi synch device when Faid motioned to him. Acolyte waved him away.

I will do it, Acolyte sent to the technician, then lock-sent to Faid, "especially if he is Jannai I cannot have that on someone else's head.**

Faid nodded, he understood. Acolyte went to the back of the Forward Base, went into a cabinet, took out the inject gun and the other items he would need to jack Blue.

What type of jack do you want? asked Acolyte as Blue sat down in the psi synch device.

The same as Faid, Blue sent.

Acolyte changed the nanomachine setup on the inject gun and brought it over to the chair. He put his hand up to Faid's head and checked out his jack again just to make sure. He took the strap and anchored Blue's head to the back of the chair. He then shaved a small patch of Blue's hair and took the drill and drilled the hole in his head above his temple on the right side. Blue did not scream he just held on tight to the armrests of the chair. Acolyte put the inject gun up to Blue's head, pulled the trigger and fired it. The nanomachines started to build the jack.

You will teach me how to use it, sent Blue.

Faid was tired of Blue's manipulation. This was wearing on their relationship. Faid was not used to having to take orders from Blue. Faid had always been the one in control of their relationship. The jack continued to build. Unlike Lino's jack, Blue's jack would be the latest technology and could be upgraded like Faid's if need be. Acolyte pulled the inject gun out of Blue's head and then put another device to his head.

The jack had already configured, he just had to remove the nanomachines now. He took the other device down and then tapped the side of Blue's head. The jack was done. Blue got up out of the chair and sent to Faid.

You are the pair lead.

Go back to the Psi Faction and I will call on you later, sent Faid.

Blue had what he came for. He would now listen to Faid and let him lead. Faid was angry at Blue. He didn't want to see him right now. Blue teleported out to the bike and rode back to the Psi Faction. He parked the bike in the garage, sent to Raven and asked him to meet him in the training room.

Chris was there when Blue came in with his motorcycle jacket on and the helmet in his hand. He put the helmet down on the table and moved a chair over to the back of the room. Chris could see the jack clearly.

"Who jacked you?" asked Chris exasperated. They had not wanted Blue jacked because it could interfere with his damper skill. He reached up and put his hand to the side of Blue's head and touched the jack. It was still sensitive in that area. Blue cringed a little as Chris slapped his hand against the silver jack and the side of his head.

Raven came in the room and wanted to know what was going on.

I need you to teach me how to use the jack, sent Blue to Raven.

"Alright," said Raven and pulled up a chair next to Chris in the back.

"First you need to be able to release the terminus," said Raven. "Just think about it and it should release."

Blue successfully released the cable and it swung around and then he moved it with his mind and attached to the terminal port.

"Okay," said Raven. He had expected that to have been hard for Blue but he got it. "Now inline with the machine."

Blue could see the security screen come up on the terminal. He sent his psi into the machine through the jack and was able to bypass the first three levels of security. He then cycled through the screens and brought it up to the hangar screens and located his Quadrion schematic file. He punched up the file and started reading the data.

"You don't need my help at all," said Raven.

It had been three weeks since Blue had received his jack. Blue, Raven, and Lino were transferred to the front. They were Quadrion pilots and Gailen was their commander. Lino asked Faid to come with him. Faid had started to receive frame training at the Psi Faction. He had learned how to fly the machine but was still a weak pilot. Jai was left to run the Psi Faction and keep an eye on Chris. Gloughster and Saya were also asked to stay back. A shuttle came to pick up Gailen and Faid while Raven, Blue and Lino in their mobile frames escorted the shuttle to the battleship Escalon in the Aelean Sea.

The frames came into the hangar bay. The shuttle landed on the deck. Blue had jacked in to his frame and learned to pilot it assisted by the jack inline. Like Lino's frame, Blue's Quadrion was equipped with an all around synch that he could use to fly the machine but he had been instructed by Gailen to learn and use the jack inline so that he could be a better pilot.

Lino climbed onto the rope ladder and it lowered him to the deck from the frame cockpit. He went up to Blue and Raven and they met with an officer and he escorted them to the Ready Room. Faid met them there. They hovered around the officer who brought them. They were still holding their helmets and had their flightsuits on.

Four pilots were gathered in the back of the Ready Room and had seen Raven, Blue, Lino and Faid come in.

"Who are the new guys?" someone asked.

"I think they come from the Psi Faction if I understand correctly."

"What is up with the one with the red hair? He has an attitude. And what is he wearing? Is that a Packrat outfit?"

"You don't even know him. Where does that come from?"

"Did you hear that those two are coming?"

"Who?"

"The Isshin pilots."

"Those crazy bastards are coming here?"

"Yes, they are."

"I don't want to fly with them."

"I hear one of the Psi Faction guys is going to be flying an Isshin too."

"He must be an Ace then."

"I wonder which one of them it is."

"I hope it is not the red haired guy."

"Break it up," said Fred coming over to the group of pilots and waving them off. Fred was the squadron leader that would be hosting the Isshin pilots when they came in.

Fred walked up to Blue and the group with Jane. The officer acknowledged Fred and introduced him to the Psi Faction group.

"This is Fred Thompson. He will be the Isshin pilot squadron lead. This is his mate pair Jane Elliot."

"Nice to meet you," said Raven bowing.

"Fred will show you to your quarters. Are any of you mate pairs?" asked the officer.

"I am mate pair to Faid," said Blue.

"Then we will arrange you to be in the same room."

Fred showed them down the hall. The ship was bigger than Lino had thought it would be. Fred took them around the corner and brought them to an area with a lot of people hanging around. Fred and Jane both had jacks as it seemed did all the other pilots.

"That is the cafeteria," said Fred as the door opened and someone came out. They walked past the cafeteria and then went down the corridor into the living quarters.

Ameliano, you will be in this room alone. Raven you are across the hall you have a roommate. Blue and Faid you are right next door," said Fred.

"When do we need to report?" asked Raven.

"0800 hours tomorrow morning report to the Ready Room. There will be a mission briefing. Faid you still have training. Ameliano I need you to come with me now. Your team should be in shortly."

Lino opened the door and put his helmet down on the bed and followed Fred back down the hall. Fred was taller than Lino and more muscular. Lino looked like a kid. Fred's jack was red like a lot of the other pilots. It was a military jack.

"We need to test your reaction time. We would like you to go up in the simulator so we can see what you can do."

Fred walked back with Lino to the hangar. The simulator view was piped into the Ready Room. A lot of the pilots had come to the Ready Room to see the simulation with Lino. Fred led Lino over and he sat down in the simulator and it raised up off the floor on shocks. Fred handed Lino a pin drive that he put into the ignition. Lino keyed in the start up procedure on the simulator and released his jack and jacked in. He settled his feet on the pedals. The screener took some points off his simulation start up score for not jacking in before he did the start up procedure. He moved his feet on the pedals testing it out and it moved the simulator flaps. He put his hands through the stirrup controls and the heads up display came up. It looked real. A voice came over the console and told him to start.

Lino took off. He could see his movement through the heads up display. Immediately there were bandits on him from the front. He banked and went past them. The pilots in the Ready Room were watching the simulated battle. Lino transformed the plane into a frame and reversed direction instantly and went after the first bandit. He swerved around in front of it and fired the guns and hit the plane and it went up in smoke and fell off the view. The alarm came on, someone was on him. He reversed direction again, transformed and flew off trying to shake the attacker. He flew low and slowed down so that his attacker would get closer.

"Why is he slowing down?" asked one of the pilots in the Ready Room.

"He is trying to bring them in closer."

Lino moved the frame behind the attacker and blew it up with the gennen rifle and then went back to re-engage. He flew fast into the group that had been on him before and banked, then transformed again and released the gennen rifle and fired in a 360 degree radius and took out 6 of the pursuers and then transformed and flew off. The proximity alarm came on again. Lino couldn't see where it was coming from. He transformed and the attacker came directly at him and fired on him. Lino kept himself from getting hit. He took out the sword module and went after the attacker and they got into a close combat battle. Lino swung at the attacker and it hit the cockpit and blew up.

Four frames came at him and started firing. Lino took out the rifle and fired behind each of the frames until he hit them all.

"How can he move like that," said one of the pilots in the Ready Room.

"His tactics are crazy. He is like faster than the simulator," said another pilot.

Three other attackers came at Lino in his frame configuration. Lino transformed, they transformed right behind him. The simulator was learning from Lino's tactics. They chased him. Lino started to dive straight toward the ground.

"What, is he crazy? He is going to lose," said another pilot watching the simulated battle.

Lino ran his plane directly to the ground and then transformed and hovered. The simulated planes crashed into the ground. The simulation was over.

Lino stepped out of the simulator. Blue and Faid came walking up. Fred put his hand on Lino's shoulder.

"We would like you to fly the Quadrion Isshin."

"I have never heard of that model."

"It is a nineth-generation frame model," said Fred and led Lino over to the side of the hangar. There were frames lined up around the edges and maintenance crew walking around. He took Lino over to a black frame.

"It is black," said Lino.

"Yes, the Isshin has radar deflection that makes up part of its stealth system," said Fred and handed Lino a pin drive. "This is yours now." Lino walked up to the frame and grabbed the rope and put his foot in the stirrup and pushed the button and the rope system raised him up to the cockpit. He climbed into the cockpit and released his jack and put the pin drive in the ignition. He jacked in.

A black frame materialized in the hangar followed by another one.

"The Isshin pilots are here," someone said from behind Faid. He turned around and looked at the frames as they walked across the hangar to the staging area. Fred came up to Faid.

"You will fly Ameliano's old frame now."

Faid nodded. The pilots of the two Quadrion Isshins came out of their cockpits using the rope system and lowered down to the deck. They walked over to Fred, Faid and Blue. They were wearing black flight suits.

The taller pilot took his helmet off and flung his shoulder length blonde hair back. His head was shaved on one side and there were wires running along one side of his head coming out of his jack.

Nathaneal, sent Blue.

"That is you," said Nathaneal taking Blue's hand. "I thought so."

"You know him?" asked Faid.

"Yes, this is Nathaneal. He was one of the test subjects with me at the Psi Faction," said Blue.

"Your voice is still the same," said Nathaneal remarking on the reverberation.

The other pilot came up and took off his helment and walked up to Blue. He had an optical sensor over his eye and coming out of his jack. His hair was brown and down to his ears. He moved in close to Blue and put his forehead on Blue's and put his hands on his shoulders. They stood there like that for a while then disengaged.

"Sati," said Blue.

"It has been a long time Julian. You two are mate pairs," said Sati pointing at Faid.

"How do you know that?" asked Faid.

"He just told me," Sati put his hand back on Blue's forehead. "Nathaneal and I are mate pairs too but we have been away from each other for a while."

"They paired us and then separated us. I guess they didn't want two crazies together," laughed Nathaneal.

Lino came out of the Isshin. He had seen the other two Isshin pilots arrive. He wanted to meet them.

"I am your squadron leader, my name is…"

"You are Fred Thompson, leader of the Blue Squadron. I read about you. Where is your mate pair Jane?" asked Sati.

"She is inside. You will meet her soon. She is also in the squad with Ameliano."

"You can call me Lino," said Lino coming up to them.

"Wow, what level are you?" asked Sati. He leaned in to put his forehead on Lino's but Fred pushed him aside.

"That is rude. Levels are not supposed to be discussed in public. The levels will be posted by call number on the board after the meeting. Come with me," said Fred.

Sati and Nathaneal walked with Fred out of the hangar. There were some whispers as the two of them left. There was definitely some history there.

They separated them, sent Blue. **I think Sati has gone insane. His mind is really convoluted.**

"Their levels are high," said Faid.

Sati is level 100 from what he sent to me, sent Blue.

"I heard you can go insane with a level that high," said Lino watching them disappear through one of the many hangar doors.

"You should talk with your level where it is now," said Faid.

"That is why you are here to watch me right? Isn't that what Albion told you?"

Faid had not known that Albion had told Lino that as well. He put his hand on Blue's waist and led him away. Lino went back to the Isshin.

The flight officer finished the meeting in the Ready Room and told the pilots to go take a look at their levels on the sheets posted outside the door. Each person would have their combatant number posted with the level after it so they would not see the names. Lino already knew what his level was from being with Albion. He didn't need to look. The meeting broke up and the pilots went to the posting. There was some commotion as they could see there was someone with level 325 on the sheet.

"Who is 325? That is crazy," said one of the pilots.

"Who knows. They don't want us to find out other people's numbers for whatever reason. But 325, that person must be insane, you can't have a level that high without being loopy."

"There are two people at 100 as well."

"That is probably the Isshin pilots. Those two are crazy. I heard they had to separate them for some reason. I think they are mate pairs. They are going to go up against that new Psi Faction pilot today in a mock battle. I want to see what those three can do."

Nathaneal came up to Lino he had been looking at the sheets up on the wall. Nathaneal was really tall. There were still a group of pilots hovered over the sheets looking up their levels.

"Come with me," said Nathaneal and Lino followed him back to his cabin.

The cabin looked exactly like Lino's with two bunk beds, a window, a closet and a little desk with a laptop under the window. Nathaneal picked up his helmet off the desk and put it on the bed and then went into the closet and chucked a hyper inject syringe at Lino who could see a vial of red in it.

"I can't take red," said Lino.

"No? You feel to me like you can," said Nathaneal.

He looked at Lino awkwardly and then took out another syringe and shot himself up. Lino didn't say anything.

"You don't want them to know you are a Jannai do you," said Nathaneal.

Lino just looked away.

"It is probably better if they don't know. They will start treating you badly. Like they will do to me after I finish my next mission. Sati has been altered too. He is just like Blue."

"You mean he is..."

"Yes, Sati is just like Blue with Jannai blood. They had their conditioning done together. Sati is also a damper."

"Why were you two separated?"

"I think they didn't want to have to handle two crazies at once," laughed Nathaneal. "Come on its time to go."

Lino was a little wary about having to fight these two skilled Isshin pilots. He was new to the Isshin. He had spent the good part of yesterday getting a feel for the machine and had jacked in and tried the machine synch. The mechanics had told him about the machine synch mechanism. It made the inline faster and connected the nanomachines directly. It had kind of hurt a little when Lino had tried it, but the mechanic had said that it decreased the reaction time and made it even easier to maneuver. Lino thought he might try it out. They had removed the weapons from the Isshin frames and equipped them with simulation weapons that would fire a laser that would read the hit. They still had the sword modules. Lino had picked up a sending from Raven that he was in the Ready Room with other pilots and they were waiting to see the show. Jane would go out in her surveillance frame and relay the encounter between the three pilots.

"We're going to see a show," said one pilot.

Faid looked up at him sitting next to Blue. They had started to leave Faid alone since they knew he was new to the frame and not a threat but they still teased Blue and Raven for being new to the ship.

They launched the three Quadrions and the Jane's frame launched after them and followed them to the sortie point. They were still close to land so there were no Atlantic

Federation carriers in the area. They would get to open water soon.

The frames had transformed to get to the sortie point and were in aircraft mode until they reached their destination. Sati's frame hung back and tailed Lino as they came on their destination.

"He's starting already," said one of the pilots in the Ready Room watching the streaming feed.

The alarm went off in Lino's frame. Sati had him right in the line of fire and had armed the laser.

"Crap," Lino transformed the frame and moved the frame behind Nathaneal's machine and tried to take him out but he was in the wrong position. Nathaneal banked and got out of the way. Sati came in again. Lino transformed and went wailing off and Sati followed him. He took Sati and Nathaneal into the mountains. They were on him tight. He couldn't shake them. Lino went up vertical out of the mountains and Nathaneal followed him. Sati took a moment and then went after him. They were working together to team up on Lino. Nathaneal got closer and got a lock. Lino raced forward, then stopped and turned transforming his frame and taking the shot. It hit Nathaneals' tail but was not a big enough read to count.

Nathaneal's frame vanished. Lino looked around for it but couldn't find him. Then Sati was on him coming straight at him the gun leveled. The frame was half transformed. The arms were out underneath the cockpit holding the rifle but the wings were still deployed. He started firing but Lino kept teleporting the frame so he couldn't get a lock on him.

"Damn you," Sati screamed and then sent a psi surge at Lino. It shocked him and he lost it for a moment.

"They got him?" asked the pilot behind Faid's shoulder. Blue could hardly believe the type of flying he was seeing. Lino's frame had a red circle on the nose when it was in its aircraft mode different than Sati's yellow and Nathaneal's blue, that is how you could tell them apart but not when they were in frame mode.

"No, he's still in it. They probably just spooked him," said another pilot.

Lino hadn't known they were going to play like that. Lino sent a psi surge back at Sati whose hand gripped the controls tight as the plane started to spin. He had lost the synch in response to the psi surge. Sati transformed and came out of it and went back after Lino. He switched to the sword module and attacked Lino's frame head on. Lino transformed and took out his sword module and started to hack away at Sati. Nathaneal kept out of it and just hovered over the two of them battling it out. The sword module did not count. It had to be a hit with the simulated laser. Sati just wanted to get back at Lino for throwing him off. The two frames went at each other ferociously. Lino hacked into the leg of Sati's frame and the sword module got stuck. Lino released it and flew off. Sati's frame extracted the sword and threw it away. Nathaneal transformed and went after Lino who climbed, the g-forces starting to affect him. He was going straight up. Nathaneal sucked in a breath trying to withstand the g-forces and chased him. Nathaneal couldn't keep up with Lino's speed. He started to slow down. Lino transformed into frame mode, stopped in mid air hovering, took out the laser and fired. The lost indicator appeared on the screen in the Ready Room as he hit Nathaneal's machine.

"Out of there," said the pilot next to Faid and clapped his hands.

Lino transformed back into aircraft mode and raced off towards the mountains. Sati followed him. They engaged low. The surveillance frame went up so that it could still see the battle. Sati's frame clipped its wing in the mountains. The plane wobbled and then he broke off his pursuit and climbed. Lino was crazy flying at that speed through obstacles. Lino broke off his trajectory, and went after Sati.

The alarm came on in Sati's cockpit. Lino had locked on to him. Lino gave chase. Sati flew away fast then started teleporting the frame as he went so that Lino couldn't get a lock.

"Come on," Lino said out loud chasing him down. Sati transformed and took out its sword module and hit Lino's plane on the nose as it was going by. It sharply dipped and then Lino transformed and came out of a dangerous situation.

"Those two are crazy," said another pilot in the Ready Room watching the battle.

Lino pulled out the second sword module and attacked Sati again. They were wildly going at each other. Suddenly

Sati's frame vanished and disappeared into the clouds and set up the shot. Lino couldn't see from the sun. Sati's plane came half transformed out of the clouds and took the shot as he went by and got him.

Its over! sent Sati angrily. He zoomed past Lino on the way back to the ship. Lino was defeated. Lino returned to base.

In the hangar Sati pulled off his helmet and walked quickly up to Lino who had just left the cockpit and Sati threw his helmet down on the ground, took Lino by the collar and punched him in the face.

Fred ran over but Sati already had Lino.

"You clipped my Isshin," Sati pulled Lino behind him and pushed him towards his frame. There was a huge gash in the leg where Lino had hit the frame with his frame's sword module.

"They can repair that," said Lino.

"No, it hurt!" screamed Sati and then shoved Lino hard and picked up his helmet, storming off. Nathaneal came up to Lino and put his hand on his shoulder.

"What was that all about?" asked Lino.

"Sati was machine synched. He was inline with the machine so it hurt him when you inflicted that damage," said Nathaneal.

Lino looked back at Sati and could see that he was limping. He had his hand on his thigh as he walked away. Lino looked over at Sati's frame.

"Go to the Ready Room so you can debrief," said Fred.

Sati threw himself down in a chair in the Ready Room. There were still pilots there who had seen the battle from the surveillance frame feed. They hovered around Sati because he had won the battle. Nathaneal and Lino came into the Ready Room and sat down to the left of Sati. The officer came in who was going to debrief them.

"Everyone out just Ima, Barjan and Dejarre," said the officer. The rest of the pilots cleared out.

"They are going to get yelled at," said one of the pilots as he left and closed the door behind him.

The officer made sure the door was closed before he started in on them. He stood behind the podium and put his hands on the top and clasped them together.

"That was reckless..." said the officer.

"Who me?" asked Nathaneal.

"No Dejarre. You fly my plane through mountains at mach what-have-you and you think that plane is yours? That is my machine. You do that crap in simulation but you do not fly my plane like that. You could have killed yourself. Do you know how much that frame costs?" yelled the officer.

Lino shook his head and opened his mouth to speak.

"Don't talk, just listen. You two are not off the hook either. They transferred you back here because you are loose cannons. You do not own those frames. Your Jannai blood does not get you a free pass. You have to do it better and faster than these two," the officer said pointing at Nathaneal. "Now get out of here," the officer waved them off.

Lino, Sati and Nathaneal left the Ready Room. Sati was still limping. Sati and Lino went back to the locker room. Nathaneal gave Sati his helment and went to the cafeteria. Sati pulled off his flight suit and put on his military uniform. He had a large bruise on his thigh.

"Wow, you really did get hurt. I did not know the machine synch could do that," said Lino as Sati pulled up his pants.

"It is the nanomachines," said Sati and buckled his pants.

Lino pulled on his shirt and buttoned it up and tucked it into his pants. They had actually found his correct size. Sati was thin like Lino.

"Are you a neurocyne addict? They frown on that in the military," said Sati. He was looking at Lino's hands and the freckles on his cheeks.

"Yes, I went psi crit and went past my limit."

"Did you come with Blue?"

"Yes, we were at the Psi Faction together with Raven."

"I've seen you before," said Sati looking up at him. He sat down on the bench to put on his shoes. The shoes were black like their uniforms.

"Yes, I have been on the newsfeed before."

"No way!" said Sati really loud, standing up and pointing at him. There were other people in the locker room who looked over at him. "You're the Viceroy aren't you? They stabbed you. I saw that. You healed yourself," Sati came up and patted Lino on the stomach.

"Get off me," said Lino pushing him off. The rest of the people in the room turned towards them and looked at Lino and started to whisper.

"Did he stab you hard?"

"No, it wasn't deep," said Lino.

"And you are an Isshin pilot. Where is your Trance Channeler?"

"He is back at the Psi Faction with his Adept."

"He is your mate pair, right?" asked Sati who was being a little over familiar and Lino didn't like it very much. He was also using very informal language with Lino like he had been friends with him for years. "Don't you miss not being around him? It virtually drove me insane to not be able to see Nathaneal."

Someone walked past Sati and called him insane. Sati put his hands behind his head and just laughed.

"Ameliano Dejarre please come to the Command Center," came over the intercom.

Lino walked out of the locker room and left Sati there. Lino didn't really know his way around yet. He had to ask a few people how to get to the Command Center. He had to take a staircase. There was a large window that showed the landing pad of the battleship. Gailen motioned him to come in. Lino walked over to him.

"The Captain wanted to meet the Viceroy," said Gailen leading Lino over.

The Captain got up out of his seat and saluted Lino who saluted back.

"It is nice to have the representative of the Pacific Territories as part of our team. I hear you have joined the Blue Squadron as an Isshin pilot. That is an elite position," said the Captain.

"Yes sir," said Lino.

Chapter 2

They gave Blue a squadron lead position. Raven was in his squad with three other pilots. Faid was still being trained and had been assigned a training detail so he would not be flying for a while, just simulation. Blue went to the cafeteria with Nathaneal. There were whispers as he walked by.

It started already, sent Nathaneal to Blue who looked out into the sea of green uniforms. Only the Isshin pilots had black uniforms.

Nathaneal got in line behind Blue. When it was his turn at the cook he asked for Selat. The cook looked at him and left, returning with a plastic container with a cover and put it on his tray. Blue continued down the line and got some rice and pickled vegetables.

"You don't eat meat?" asked Nathaneal.

I try not to, sent Blue.

They walked back over to Sati and Lino who were seated at the long tables at the end. As Nathaneal sat down some of the people around the table in that area all got up and took their trays and went to sit somewhere else.

"Idiots," said Sati glaring at the people as they went and sat down at another table. Nathaneal straddled the seat and opened the plastic dish. Blue looked in the dish. Whatever it was looked disgusting.

"What is that?" asked Blue. Lino looked over at it.

"It is Selat. It is raw meat in sauce. It is a Jannai dish. Do you want some?" Lino held up the dish to Lino.

"Shut up," said Lino under his breath. Lino did want some but he was not about to take it. He was drinking a protein shake. He was sticking to the supplemental nutrition since he really couldn't eat regular food any more.

Faid came and joined them. His shirt was half sticking out of his pants and he looked disheveled.

"What happened to you?" asked Sati.

"I had to help the maintenance crews move some equipment," sadi Faid. They had tried to get him to cut his hair earlier and he had declined so they made him work for it.

Nathaneal put his hand in the plastic dish and pulled out a piece of meat and put it in his mouth.

"Use a fork," said Sati and handed him a fork. "You want them to also think you are an animal?"

Nathaneal's eyes flashed. He took the fork and stabbed it into the disk. The Isshin pilots had a mission coming up today. They would be infiltrating the Atlantea Federation carrier to get information about their strategic capacity. Lino would pilot with Sati, and Nathaneal would be going in. Lino still didn't know how Nathaneal was going to get into the carrier. He didn't look like a Jannai.

Faid touched Blue on the shoulder as he got up. Another pilot with a higher rank came over and tapped Faid on the chest and told him to fix his uniform. Faid did as he was told.

"Parat is coming up," said Faid as he walked away.

Why does he keep reminding me of that? sent Blue.

"Don't you know what Parat is?" asked Nathaneal.

"No, actually I don't," said Blue.

"Have you done it yet?" asked Sati.

Blue looked embarrassed.

"No."

"Is he making you wait then for the holiday?" asked Sati.

"Parat is the joining holiday. If you were just joined it will be a big deal. You get off from practice on that day too," said Nathaneal.

"You are going to get boinked," said Sati and started to laugh.

"What about you? Aren't you mate pairs?" asked Blue.

"We don't do that religious crap," said Sati. "That is a Packrat thing. How did you hook up with a Packrat anyway? And where did you get a hacker jack from?"

"The Packrats jacked me," said Blue.

"When did you become a terrorist?" asked Sati.

"I am not a terrorist," said Blue angrily and sparked up his aegis.

Sati and Blue had a very volatile relationship. Sati had been jealous of Blue when they were at the Psi Faction back as test subjects. The officer who had chided Faid came over to Blue and put his hand on his shoulder and told him to calm down. Blue put his aegis out.

"Isshin pilots please report to the hangar," came over the intercom.

Nathaneal, Lino and Sati got up and left Blue in the cafeteria. Lino went back to his room first before he went to the hangar.

"You are late," said Fred as Lino walked up to the group in the hangar. Jane, Sati and Nathaneal were there.

Jane handed Nathaneal a Jannai Atlantea Federation uniform. "This is what you need to wear."

Fred went about explaining the mission to them. Lino was going to be the pilot. Sati had to go so that Nathaneal could teleport on his signal. They would take the captured Quadrion Solstice with a pilot, nav and gunner seat.

"Go get set up. You leave in an hour."

Nathaneal put on the Jannai uniform and walked back with Sati and Lino through the halls. The pilots looked at Nathaneal as they passed through the hangar. There were some sneers and comments.

The three of them climbed the ramp and the ramp raised them up to the frame cockpit. Nathaneal's eyes flashed and then he put his hands on Sati's shoulders to stabilize himself and he changed. His skin became white and he grew fangs. The irises of his eyes changed and he grew scales on his face. He looked like a Jannai warrior. It had hurt him to change. Lino just looked at him. He had no idea.

"Come on," said Sati.

Nathaneal looked over the side of the ramp and could see the mechanics looking up at him and pointing. He looked like a Jannai now. The taunting would get worse. Lino and Sati climbed into the frame. Nathaneal moved behind Sati's seat. Lino closed the cockpit and started up the ignition sequence. The catapult launched the frame and it cruised into open air. They would meet up with the Atlantea Federation fleet, join the formation and then Nathaneal would teleport out into the ship.

It took a good two hours to come up on the Atlantea Federation fleet. The lead battle cruiser pinged the frame and Nathaneal spoke in Jannai, gave the IFF code and they accepted it. They were requested to join the formation.

"This is dangerous," said Lino as he flew the frame into formation behind the carrier. "How are we going to get out of here?"

"You are going to teleport us out," said Nathaneal.

"Are you kidding me? The frame and two additional people, you are going to kill me."

"That is why your level is 325, right?"

Lino didn't say anything. How did they know that.

"We can feel you. It has to be you," said Sati.

Lino got in formation and then Nathaneal teleported out onto the ship. He materialized in a hallway. He had to get his bearings. They had been briefed. The Atlantea Federation carrier was the same class so the ship was laid out in a similar manner. He needed to find the server room. He asked a Jannai in the hallway who directed him down the corridor. Nathaneal walked to the server room and went in. They paid him no mind as he jacked in at the back terminal. There were about five Jannai administrators in the room. He had to get past the security first, which was not hard to do. He put his hands down on the keyboard. A Jannai came up to him and asked him his designation. He made something up and luckily it was accepted. The Jannai left him alone. Nathaneal punched up the strategic command file, found the troop formations and the strategic strength of the Atlantea Federation fleet as well as other data.

He jacked out and got up and walked out of the server room. No one followed him out. He passed some Jannai in the hall and waited until he was clear and then teleported back to the frame and materialized in Sati's lap. He had teleported to Sati's signal. Since they were mate pairs he used Sati as his anchor point. He moved back into the gunner seat.

"Okay. Let's get out of here," said Sati.

Lino closed his eyes and teleported the frame back to the hangar. It materialized in the center of the hangar. Lino opened the cockpit. He had to power down and perform the shut down procedure. The mechanics moved the ramp over to the frame and Sati and Nathaneal got down out of the frame. Nathaneal changed back when they got on the ground. Everybody saw him. Sati walked with him out of the hangar. Nathaneal had to go to the Command Center to download the data. The Captain wanted it done directly where he could see him. Nathaneal jacked in and unloaded the data at a terminal at the back. There was a guard put on him. He finished the data transfer and the guard accompanied him back to his room where Sati was waiting for him.

"It is going to start now," said Nathaneal.

"They don't know any better," responded Sati softly.

Nathaneal left the room and went back to the cafeteria. Someone tried to trip him in the hall. Nathaneal's metabolism was very fast. He had to eat every few hours or he was starving and could get sick. His Jannai blood was pure like Lino's but he had been infused like Blue and Sati. He got the same thing he had before. It took them some time to make it. He waited at the counter for them. Faid was in the cafeteria by himself.

Nathaneal went to sit down at the end of the long table. He put his tray on the table. The entire table got up and walked away. Faid saw this and stood up and went to sit with him.

"You don't have to," said Nathaneal. He didn't even look up at Faid as he sat down. Faid sat there silent for awhile and just watched Nathaneal eat with his hands.

"Why don't you at least try…" said Faid.

"Because it is not worth the effort. They are going to shun me anyway. I t was just a matter of time. This happens everywhere. They use me because they can and then I have to deal with this."

"How did they make it so you could change like that?" Faid asked. He had not been in the hangar but he had heard.

"It was the amount of red they fed me when I was at the Psi Faction," said Nathaneal.

"But you were infused like Blue, right?"

"It was basically the same, a little different actually. They did it gradually not like Blue and Sati, that they did all at once during their conditioning. I think it made it so that I had a higher tolerance to the drug."

Chapter 3

"The Dionysis Air Fortress is coming here?" asked Gailen to the Captain in the Command Center.

"That is what it looks like," said an officer leaning over the radar officer's shoulder.

"We don't have the command strength to take that thing out," said another officer.

"We may be able to wage a strike attack with a small force and take it out from the inside."

"But there are kedek shields," said Gailen.

"You are familiar with the fortress?"

"One of the Psi Faction pilots has been inside the fortress for another mission," said Gailen.

"Then we can use his expertise," said the Captain. "Call a meeting and get him in there. I want his inputs on this.

Gailen went about making the preparations.

Nathaneal spent the rest of the morning in his cabin. He did not want to deal with the taunting. Sati had tried to get him to come with him but Nathaneal had blown off the ops meeting and just hid. He didn't want to deal with it right now. He would have to go to the cafeteria. He was saving up his strength. He was irritated this morning. Fred had come to see him and they talked it over.

"You can't let them get to you," said Fred in Nathaneal's cabin.

"You walk around here with that stigma and tell me that again," Nathaneal sparked up his aegis to his hands.

"You know you need to calm down. Get a hold of yourself."

"I've had enough of this," said Nathaneal.

Fred left the cabin and went to the officer's lounge. He had a meeting with Gailen.

"The Isshin pilots are restless," said Fred sitting down in the back at a table with two lounge chairs. Gailen was already there.

"We need Lino to be available for a meeting about the Dionysis Air Fortress. Nathaneal will be asked to go in again," said Gailen.

"I don't think he is emotionally ready to handle that with the other members of the team."

"The other Isshin pilots are against him?" asked Gailen.

"No, I don't think that is the problem. I think his Jannai blood is spooking the other pilots," said Fred. He put his hand up to his chin.

Gailen crossed his legs and looked out into the room. There was another officer reading the newspaper.

"Sati and Blue have Jannai blood as well," said Gailen.

"I don't know if this is it. It could be his jack and the fact that he is really tall. He is tall enough to be a Jannai warrior. I think we need to have him change out of sight the next time."

"You have a point. We can't have him completely shunned by the rest of the crew."

Nathaneal left his cabin and went to the cafeteria. He had started to feel sick because he hadn't eaten. They had trained the cooks to make two Jannai dishes since he had to eat a specific type of food to maintain his health. That had also caused some turmoil with the kitchen staff. He walked up to the counter with a tray and they just went to the back and gave him what they had. They were not going to make something special for him. They just rotated the menu. Nathaneal did not complain, took the plastic dish and walked to a small table. He sat in the corner of the long aisle so he didn't inconvenience the rest of the crew. He was eating with his hands peacefully and then someone came up behind him and dumped a bowl of stew on his head. Nathaneal stood up slowly and turned towards the guy and sent him careening against the wall with his psi. The guy got up and ran at Nathaneal who pulled a gun and pointed it at the guy.

"You cannot have a loaded gun in here," said an officer and stood up and walked over to Nathaneal.

"You are crazy," said the guy.

The officer pulled the gun out of Nathaneal's hand and called the MP over who took Nathaneal's hands behind his back and cuffed him. They led him out of the cafeteria.

"Serves you right crazy bastard," said the guy who had the gun pointed at him.

"He could have killed you," said a pilot close to him.

Gailen continued talking to Fred. An officer came into the lounge and came up to Fred and told him they had Nathaneal in custody. Gailen gave Fred leave to go. Fred walked to the detention hold.

Nathaneal still had stew in his hair when Fred came up to the cell they were holding him in.

"What happened?" Fred asked.

"Someone dropped food on me and I pulled a gun on him."

"You can't walk around with a loaded gun," said Fred.

"I was protecting myself."

"You have been written up for that before at your last station. You can't be doing that. Get up."

Fred went to the side of the detention block and went into

a cabinet and took out a towel and handed it to Nathaneal through the bars. Nathaneal wiped his head and shoulders to get the food off. There was a guard in the detention block. Fred waved the guard over and had him let Nathaneal out. He escorted Nathaneal back to his room.

"If that happens again report it."

Nathaneal agreed but was not about to do that.

The battleship Escalon left the Aelean Sea and traveled into the Atlantic Ocean. The Pacific Territories' battleship was accompanied by two other battleships, three smaller boats and a barge. They scrambled the frame pilots. There was a lot of activity in the hangar. Blue's squadron was sent out early on with the rest of the frames. The Isshin pilots were held back because there were some concerns about a specific squadron that was supposedly with the Atlantea Federation fleet.

Lino, Sati and Nathaneal were waiting to launch in their frames. The Atlantea Federation Isshin pilots were confirmed in the battle group. Lino's and Sati's frames were launched off catapult one. Then the catapult broke so that Nathaneal couldn't launch. Catapult two was already broken from the previous launches and was being repaired.

Lino and Sati went supersonic and got into the fray. The Atlantea Federation Isshin pilots engaged Lino and Sati. They were outnumbered. Sati half transformed his Isshin and took out the gennen rifle and started shooting. Lino transformed and received a sending from someone. His proximilty alarm went off. Someone was on him.

Sati came over Lino's comm." Be careful. That is the Streak" Sati knew the markings on that Atlantea Federation frame.

Lino flew past the main fleet but the pilot in the Streak was on him tight. He half transformed and went after the Streak with the gennen rifle. The Streak kept teleporting and Lino could not get the shot. The pilot in the Streak sent to Lino again and threw him off.

I am going to claim your death, came the awkward sending. This was a Jannai pilot. The Streak let Lino get in close, then swiveled and hit Lino's frame in the leg. Sati could see Lino engaged with the Streak Isshin and went to assist him. The Streak had shot Sati down once, and he remembered. The Streak transformed and took out two rifle modules and started spinning in the air firing wildly. The Streak hit Sati's frame and he was out of it. He had to return to the ship. He sent to Lino to be careful of the Streak's bank left maneuver.

The Streak transformed and came at Lino forcing him to fly off holding the gennen rifle underneath the wings. He would not be able to run as fast. He put up the rifle and transformed back to full aircraft mode and ran. The Streak chased him.

A voice came over Lino's comm that he was out too far. Lino banked and transformed. The Streak transformed and went after Lino with the sword module. The Streak banked left and came at Lino and struck the cockpit. It hit the cockpit door. It shocked Lino. The Streak came in again with the sword module over its head and stabbed the sword module into the cockpit. The sword module hit Lino and pinned him to the seat. Lino's frame started to fall out of the sky.

Lino could not transform the sword module was sticking out of the cockpit. Lino teleported away. The Streak still had his signal and went after him. The Streak backed off the closer Lino got to the battleship. Lino teleported the frame into the hangar. He lowered the frame onto its knees. Nathaneal and Sati saw the state of the frame. The mechanics brought the ramp over. Nathaneal got up on the ramp. The mechanics called to Lino over the radio but he did not respond. They raised the ramp up to the cockpit. A frame came over and extracted the sword module from Lino's Isshin.

Lino released the seat harness and took off his helmet. He didn't know if he could move. The sword module had pinned him to the seat. The mechanics plugged in the Isshin at the leg port to the maintenance module and opened the cockpit. Nathaneal leaned in and put out his hand. He could see Lino's eyes glowing. There was a huge gash through his stomach where the sword module had hit him. He had his hand on his stomach and it was glowing. He was trying to heal himself. There was blood all over the seat on the floor.

"Can you get up?" asked Nathaneal who put his hand on the side of the cockpit and leaned in. Lino didn't move. Nathaneal could see Lino's eyes lit up. He started to talk to Lino in Jannai. Lino was desperately trying to heal himself. He registered what Nathaneal was saying and put his hand out. Nathaneal leaned in and pulled him out. Lino's knees buckled, Nathaneal had to hold him up. The blood was staining his flight suit. His eyes were completely lit up and his hand against his stomach was glowing brightly. Nathaneal held Lino up as he came onto the ramp.

Lino gripped Nathaneal's shirt. Blood was dripping on the ramp. He needed to heal himself. Lino was critically wounded. The ramp started to lower. A medical technician came into the hangar towards the Isshin. Lino focused all his energy on healing himself. His hand glowed brighter. He needed more power. Lino screamed at the top of his lungs and his wings flung out his back and he hung onto Nathaneal's shirt tighter healing himself. The surge of power that Nathaneal felt was incredible. Sati could feel it from where he was. Lino's eyes flashed on and off and he removed his hand and looked down at his stomach. The wound had closed. Lino's eyes stopped glowing. He retracted his wings as the ramp came to rest on the hangar floor and collapsed unconscious.

Gailen had run out of the Command Center to the hangar. He came up to Lino as the medical technicians were placing him on the stretcher. He was out cold. The mechanics and pilots in the hangar were whispering. They had all seen Lino's wings. They had seen the sword module sticking out of the frame. The entire seat in the cockpit was soaked in blood. They would have to repair the damage to the frame.

Gailen walked with Lino as the medical team carried him through the hallway on the stretcher. The word had spread quickly that Lino was a Jannai and that he had healed himself. Sati raised the ramp and climbed up into Lino's Isshin and looked inside. There was blood all over the cockpit. The seat had a large gash in it from where the sword module had pinned Lino to the seat. It was a wonder he was still alive. The sword module should have cut him in half. Fred came over to Nathaneal and told him the catapult was ready and they wanted him to launch. The mechanics had seen to Sati's Isshin. It was good to go. He would go up again. The two of them launched and went back to the battle.

Nathaneal's and Sati's frame had been damaged from the last flight and Lino's was still down for repair. It had been one week since the initial battle with the Atlantea Federation. The fleets were out in the open sea.

Gailen was in the Command Center. An officer was looking through night vision binoculars out the main window. Blue's squadron was out on a night run. Lino's old frame had been equipped with surveillance equipment and Faid had gone out with Blue's squad as the trail.

"Keep it tight," came Blue's voice over Faid's comm link. Faid had been drifting back. The radar sensor was spinning above the frame in aircraft mode. There was no activity out where they were right now. Faid took the opportunity to talk to Blue.

"Parat is tomorrow," said Faid over the comm.

"You two need to stop," came Raven.

"You have been talking about that for the last week," said Blue his voice reverberating over the comm.

"What is Parat again?" came the third pilot in Blue's squadron.

"It is the mate pair joining holiday," said Faid.

"Oh yeah, you are a Packrats aren't you?" asked the pilot.

"Cut the chatter," came Gailen over the comm. He was on the radio frequency.

A signal came over Faid's machine. They were tracking something. Faid looked at his instruments and tapped on the panel.

"You have something in the water," said Faid over the comm. The command center on the Escalon confirmed there was something under water. They scrambled the submersible frames.

"We are getting low on fuel," radioed in Blue.

"RTB," came the response.

Blue turned his squadron around and sent them back. The frames transformed back to frame mode to land so they did not need the catch.

"You are too low," said the cat operator over the comm as Faid came in. Faid was coming in aircraft mode so he would need to catch the cable with the tail hook. They had put surveillance apparatus on the frame so that it could not transform,

"Pull up," said the cat operator.

"Call the ball."

"I have the ball," said Faid. He was a little nervous each time he did this. He came in with the tail hook down and it scraped against the deck and caught the metal cabling stopping the plane. He clasped his hands together and taxied the frame to the ramp, retracting the wings and the ramp lowered down into the hangar. The landing area was in between the catapults that were against the outsides of the deck. The ramp lowered down with Faid's frame and he went through the shutdown procedure once they got into the hangar.

Lino was in his room alone. A knock came on the door. Lino opened the door and four pilots rushed him and threw him down on the bed. One of them put his hands over Lino's mouth.

"Friggin' Jannai," said one of the pilots.

Lino struggled under their hold but he was not about to use his psi against them.

"You're the one with the level, aren't you?" said another pilot. "I can feel you. Abomination."

They tied his hands and feet and put tape over his mouth and started to punch him in the stomach.

"We don't need any more Jannai. You are a disgrace."

Lino sent into their minds.

"Psi Faction scum. You think I want you in my mind. You are just like Nathnaeal. You are crazy too."

One of the pilots hit him in the face and knocked Lino out. They ripped up his room and left. Lino came to a while later and broke the restraints with his psi and got up. He went over to the closet and opened the door, and looked at his face in the mirror. He might get a black eye. He didn't know.

He went to the cafeteria. He was slightly doubled over. His stomach hurt. The crowd parted as he walked by and the whole room went silent. He had been in the infirmary for a few days and had just been let out since they wanted to make sure that he really was healed. Lino went up to the cook and ordered Selat. He didn't give a crap now, they knew. His eyes flashed as he walked to the table and sat down with Sati and Nathaneal.

"So they got you too?" asked Sati putting his hand up to Lino's cheek. The bruising was starting to show. Sati had been there with Nathaneal when Lino had released his wings.

A pilot walked by and called Lino inhuman as he passed. Sati stood up. Lino put his hand on Sati's arm to stop him.

"Just leave it alone," said Lino and opened the lid of the plastic container and started to eat with his hands.

"Use a fork," said Sati.

Lino tried the Selat. It was actually really good. He had been craving raw meat but had not wanted to risk it before. It didn't matter now. His eyes flashed as he ate. Nathaneal could feel his level surge as his eyes glowed.

"You've been repressing it all this time," said Sati. "That had to have been hard.

"You should be dead," said Nathaneal.

Lino wasn't hearing them. His eyes were flashing on and off.

"He's gone," said Nathaneal waving his hand in front of Lino's face. Lino didn't even register them.

"He must have been starving," said Nathaneal watching Lino eat, he was shoving the food in his mouth.

"It must have taken a lot out of him to heal himself like that. You didn't see the cockpit. That sword module went right through him." Sati put his hand on Nathaneal's forehead across the table and sent him an image of what he saw when he looked in the cockpit of Lino's Isshin.

"Wow, no way..." said Nathaneal.

Lino's nails began to grow and his eyes stopped flashing and lit up a bright glow.

"Careful," said Sati hitting Nathaneal in the arm.

Nathaneal looked over at Lino and started to speak in Jannai really low. Lino didn't register him. He raised his voice and some of the other pilots around where they were seated heard him. They got up and started remarking to the other pilots as they walked away. They wanted to get as far away from them as they could. Nathaneal raised his voice and said something really loud in Jannai. The room went silent. Lino snapped out of it and looked up.

"What happened?" asked Lino.

"You started to change," said Sati.

"Take the Jannai out of here. We don't need them. Go back to the Atlantea Federation!" said someone in the cafeteria.

The officer that had chided Faid for his uniform went up to the mechanic who said that and had the guard escort him out of the hall.

Chapter 4

They had repaired the Isshin frames from the damage they had taken at the hands of the Atlantea Federation. The fighting had been continuing for the past day. Blue's squadron had gone up twice. They had even put the squad that Faid was in on alert.

The Dionysis Air Fortress had joined its sister fleet of Atlantea Federation carriers. The Dionysis had kedek warheads. Gailen and the officers were debating how to go up against it. They had been in the meeting for over three hours. Lino was there but had not been asked to say anything at this point.

Gailen, what is the pilot's take on the shields?" The Captain turned to Lino and looked at him. Lino was not at the table. He was at the back in the seats that were lining the room.

"Ameliano Dejarre, please step up and give your inputs," said Gailen.

Lino stood up and moved to a podium that was in the room in front of the oval table around which the officers were sitting. Lino put his hands down to his sides and stood up straight. He was nervous.

"I was on the server floor. All the data is piped through that one room. It seems that you can teleport through the shields but it is not as easy getting in. I was able to teleport out by myself.

"What mission took you to the air fortress?" asked one of the officers. Gailen chimed in.

"It was a mission requested by the Emperor."

"That does not give me any information."

"We unloaded a virus program into the Dionysis that infected the main systems of their fleet while it was in the homeland," said Lino.

"How did you get into the Dionysis then if you were at the Psi Faction?" asked the Captain.

"He teleported," said Gailen.

The officers looked at Lino and he nodded.

"How can he have teleported that far?"

"Dejarre's level is very high," said Gailen.

"What is it?" asked the officer that had started the line of questioning. The Captain put his hand up. Levels were not supposed to be discussed.

"Suffice it to say..." said the Captain, "his level is high enough to be an Isshin pilot. That is enough information for me. Do you think you could go back in there if you were requested?"

"Yes sir, but I do not know how they would not be able to mistake me for an intruder," said Lino.

"Can we get a frame in there?" asked the Captain. "We could send in Nathaneal Barjan."

"You would have to hold the shields open in some fashion," said another officer.

"Thank you Dejarre. You are dismissed," said the Captain.

Lino saluted and left the room. He was just happy to get out of there. He had worn his Isshin dress uniform and pulled the shirt out of his pants on the way back to his room. The uniform had a lot of starch in it and it itched. He wanted to take it off. He changed his clothes back to his regular uniform and sent to Blue who was in the cafeteria with Faid.

When Lino got to the cafeteria, Faid and Blue were dressed in all black. There were a few other people in black as well. They must also be celebrating Parat. Lino sat down with Blue and Faid. They were sending and not speaking in observance of the holiday. Blue was eating vegetables. Faid was fasting.

Aren't you going to eat? sent Faid.

"Later," said Lino, "my stomach kind of hurts." Lino had been picking up a sending for the past hour and it was making him kind of sick. He had the urge to get in his Isshin and destroy something. He didn't know where that was coming from.

An officer dressed in all black came into the cafeteria and made an announcement, "anyone celebrating Parat please come with me."

Faid and Blue stood up as did about four other people. They went to the makeshift church that was setup in one of the larger cabins. The priest had them sit on the floor in a circle with their legs crossed. This was all new to Blue.

Faid put his hand up and made the sign of Thoth and then they listened as the priest gave them a recouting of the parable about the first joining of the god and the goddess and then he sprinkeled their heads with holy kedek water and marked a red circle on their foreheads. Blue though this was stupid but Faid was taking it seriously. Blue sent to Faid but was silenced. Faid's eyes were closed. He was listening to the priest speak about the Prophets. Blue's eyes had been glowing all day. It was a full moon.

Suddenly a sending gripped Blue. Lino, Nathaneal and Sati had the same reaction. The Streak pilot was sending to the Jannai. The sending was angry.

I want the Isshin pilots. Come... came the sending.

Nathaneal ran out of his cabin to the locker room. Sati was already there and suiting up.

The alarm went off in the ship to scramble the pilots. Blue stood up but Faid put his hand on Blue's arm and shook his head.

You do not fight today, sent Faid.

Blue sat back down and they continued the service. The priest handed each of the people a wafer that they would eat after their joining was celebrated. Faid took the wafer and cupped his hands together. The priest ended the service. Faid walked with Blue back to the room and closed and locked the door. Faid put the wafer down on the desk and told Blue to do the same. Faid started to unbutton Blue's shirt.

Lino ran down the hall to the hangar. He had gone back to his room to get his handheld. He was late again. Fred chided him as he brought his helmet and joined the group. Jane had on her flight suit. It was pink and garish. She was thin but had large breasts. Her nametag seemed to lift off her chest as she breathed. Fred's flight suit was red. He and Jane did not fly Isshins but Quadrion Excalibers. They were not as fast as the Isshin but they were lighter than the Solstice and more maneuverable.

"You will be fighting the Atlantea Federation Isshin pilots. There are 15 total," said Fred.

"They outnumber us?" asked Nathanal.

"There is only one of them we need to worry about, that Streak pilot," said Sati. His eyes were glowing.

Lino noticed that Nathaneal's eyes were glowing too.

Why are your eyes glowing? sent Lino to Sati. He stopped listening to Fred give the briefing.

It is Parat, we are mate paired and the moon is pulling at us, sent Sati.

That is why they want to fight today. The Jannai are more powerful on Parat, sent Nathaneal.

"Pay attention," said Fred, he had seen Lino and Nathaneal turn away from him. Lino apologized. His eyes were glowing as well. "I need you to concentrate and not get carried away. Try not to machine synch if you don't have to."

"Why, are you afraid we won't be able to disengage?" asked Sati.

Fred didn't say anything. He knew that Sati would synch the minute he got in the frame. That is what made him such a dangerous pilot. Lino had not tried to machine synch but he had a feeling this fight was going to be brutal and that he might need to keep the upper hand.

Fred dismissed them to their frames and they did the startup and got in position to launch. After they launched Fred came on the comm. "Do not engage until you are told." Sati's frame was moving out of formation. Fred sent to Sati to stop him from being reckless.

"There he is," said Sati over the radio as the Streak came into view. He picked up a sending from the Streak pilot.

They had launched another squadron to deal with the rest of the attackers. The Isshins would go after Streak's group. Nathaneal's frame half transformed and pulled out the gennen rifle.

"You have not been authorized," came Fred over Nathaneal's comm.

"Come on, they are right there," Nathaneal could see the frames on the heads up. Fred gave the order to transform. Sati did not. He was going after the Streak.

"Sati?" yelled Fred.

"No, I'm on him," said Sati and veered off and engaged. He blew right by the Streak and caught the Jannai in his jet wash. He was that close. The Streak pilot transformed his Isshin to stop the disturbance to his engines, transformed back, changed direction and went after Sati. Nathaneal went after them.

The Streak locked on to Sati and the alarms went off in the cockpit. Sati teleported the frame and came up behind the Streak. Another Jannai frame locked onto Nathaneal. Nathaneal's frame vanished and went up into the clouds.

Lino was engaged with three Jannai. They were on him. He kept teleporting the frame to try to keep them from locking on. He hit the machine synch button and flew off losing them. He transformed and got behind one of them and took him out with the rifle. The aircraft went into a spin and crashed into the ocean. Another Jannai Isshin that was white like the Streak came on Lino and took a shot. It clipped the leg of Lino's frame but didn't do much damage. Lino teleported behind him and took him out. Lino could see a frame on Jane. She was trying to shake them but was not having any luck. The Jannai had a lock on her. Jane was a good pilot but she was not like Sati or Nathaneal. Lino went to help her. He engaged with her pursuer and took him out.

Sati was engaged with the Streak and two other Janni frames. Sati was outnumbered and his frame was taking hits from the guns. Sati transformed and flew off. The Streak was on him. Sati flew the plane assisted by his psychic power and pulled down the keyboard and punched up the machine synch screen. An alarm rang through the cockpit. He took the limiter off the synch device.

"What are you doing?" came Fred as the warning from Sati's machine came over his screen as the squadron lead.

Sati did not answer. He pushed the keyboard out of the way and put his hands back through the stirrup controls and took back control of the plane. The Streak had come in closer and had a lock. Sati put his thumb on the button and the limiter went off. The plane zoomed forward and the Streak fell off the pursuit. It pushed Sati back in the seat. He transformed and teleported and went after the Streak. The Streak transformed and pulled out the sword module and they started to fight it out. The Streak banked left and hit Sati's frame in the cockpit. The same maneuver he had done against Lino before. He came in again for the second strike but Sati moved the frame out of the way. He was faster than the Streak pilot now with the limiter off. He hit the Streak frame across the cockpit and broke open the metal. The cockpit door shattered and Sati could see the pilot inside the frame. It was a Jannai flying the Streak. The Streak continued to attack Sati and hit the frame with the sword module and chopped off its arm. Sati felt the hit due to the machine synch. Sati's machine flew at the Streak and threw the sword and it lopped off the frame's leg. The Streak continued to advance on Sati and fired its guns and hit Sati's machine multiple times. His frame was taking a lot of damage. Another frame came out of nowhere and hit Sati's frame from behind. Sati could feel the toll it was taking on his body. He tried to disengage. He could not withstand much more of this. The Streak came at him again but Nathaneal blew by and took a shot and caught the Streak. It disengaged and flew off. The other Jannai fired and hit Sati's frame and the alarms came on. There was an error. The machine had been hit in a critical system. Sati called to Nathaneal that he was disengaging. His frame was badly beaten up.

Fred came over the comm, "go back to base."

Sati disengaged and returned to the ship. Nathaneal and Lino continued to make short work of the remaining Jannai frames. The Atlantea Federation carrier did not engage and they did not send out more planes to go up against them. Fred radioed back to base and they were called back in.

In the hangar, Sati would not come out of the frame. Nathaneal and Lino went over to Sati's Isshin. Nathaenal sent to him but got no response. Nathaneal's eyes were still lit up. Sati's frame had bullet holes throughout the external fuselage and the cockpit. Nathaneal did not know if Sati was hit or not. He picked up a sending from Sati all of a sudden.

The mechanics opened the panel in the frame's leg and plugged in the maintenace module to Sati's frame. They had to bypass the machine synch to open the cockpit door. The cockpit opened but Sati still would not come out. He couldn't jack out. The frame had taken too much damage and Sati had felt it. Sati pulled off his helmet and Nathaneal got on the ramp and raised it up to the cockpit.

"You idiot, what did you do?" said Nathaneal as he leaned into the frame.

"Nothing much, just went out for a spin," responded Satai.

"You took the limiter off, didn't you?"

Sati tapped the side of his head and tried to retract the terminus cable from his jack but it would not disengage.

"Hey, can you heal him?" called Nathaneal down to Lino.

"No, I can't heal people only myself," said Lino. Nathaneal turned back to Sati and climbed half way into the cockpit and tried to pull out the cable but it wouldn't release. He put his palm at Sati's forehead.

"Time to scream," said Nathaneal.

"I know," said Sati and gritted his teeth. Nathaneal was going to send a psi surge through Sati's body and try to knock him out. Nathaneal eyes glowed brighter as he boosted his signal and raised his power.

"This is going to hurt," said Nathaneal, his aegis sparking around his body. He sent the surge, Sati screamed. The aegis knocked out the power in the cockpit. The cable disengaged. Nathaneal leaned in and pulled Sati out of the cockpit and brought him onto the ramp. Sati was still conscious. The damage to the frame had been reflected to his body. Nathaneal laid Sati on the ramp and lowered it. He partially unzipped his flight suit at the neck and there were huge bruises on Sati's chest and neck from what he could see. The nanomachines had damaged him in the same manner as the frame had been damaged. Fred came over to see Sati lying on the ramp. Nathaneal helped Sati up to his feet and held him up. Sati's whole body hurt. His eyes were still glowing. Sati tried to take a step and faltered. Nathaneal grabbed him and held him up.

"I told you not to do that," said Fred.

"I wasn't listening, Pops," said Sati.

Fred motioned over a mechanic and told them to deactivate the synch limiter function from Sati's frame. Fred did not want him doing that again. Nathaneal helped Sati out of the hangar. They went back to their cabin. Sati sat down on the side of the bottom bunk and slowly pulled off his boots. He unzipped the flight suit and pulled it off. He was bruised from head to toe and there were what looked like bullet hole bruises on his torso in the same pattern that the frame had been hit.

"You should not have done that," said Nathaneal handing Sati a shirt and some pants. He moved slowly because his whole body hurt. He opened his mouth as he pulled on the pants and made a gasping sound.

"It was just the synch. I will recover."

"You know they told you not to do that. It can compromise your immune system," said Nathaneal.

"I don't care what they told me. It is just a machine. I need to fly."

"You don't need to be so dangerous."

"Leave me alone," said Sati standing up and walking out of the cabin.

Faid and Blue finally joined. Faid had begun to feel the effects of not consummating their mate pair relationship and it had made him sick. It was always dangerous to wait like that especially after the mate pair ceremony.

It had hurt Blue. He was lying on the bed on his stomach. Faid had been gentle but Blue's body still felt like it had just happened.

Faid took the wafer from the desk and put it in his mouth and ate it, then handed the other wafer to Blue who followed Faid's lead. He had no idea what any of this meant. Faid sat down on the corner of the bed and put his hand in Blue's hair. Blue was lying on the bed in his underware.

You rest, I will bring you something to eat, sent Faid lovingly.

Faid left the room and went down the hallway. Some of the other pilots looked at him strangely. Someone derogatorily called him a Packrat in the hall.

What of it? sent Faid. He was proud of being a Packrat. He walked into the cafeteria. He saw Sati sitting there with Raven. Faid sat down. Sati was moving very slowly. He was wearing a t-shirt and there were bruises up and down his arms and you could see them on his neck coming out of his shirt.

What happened to you? sent Faid.

"Machine synch," said Sati.

"Not a good thing to do, and he won't let me heal him either," said Raven.

Why not? sent Faid.

"Because I need to remember what losing feels like," said Sati.

"I thought you got the Streak?" asked Raven.

"I didn't get him, Nathaneal did but I think he's still out there."

What is the big deal? Just let him heal you, sent Faid. He was still not going to speak because it was Parat.

Sati was picking at his food and not really eating it. His eyes were still glowing.

"You have Jannai blood too, right?" asked Raven.

"Yes, I was infused at my conditioning just like Julian," answered Sati.

"Where is Blue?" asked Raven.

He is back in the room. He is resting, sent Faid.

"You did him, didn't you?" asked Sati.

Faid didn't say anything, just smiled.

Chapter 5

Sati refused to be healed. Fred kept him grounded until the doctors would clear him again. But that did not stop Fred from chewing Sati out for engaging before he was authorized.

"You can't just do as you like. There are protocols to follow," said Fred.

Sati just let him talk. He stood at attention in his uniform in the Ready Room. Fred had called him up in front of all the other pilots and made him stand there and take his arse chewing.

"You fly when you are told to fly and you engage when you are told to engage, not before. You were a loose cannon at your last station and that is why they sent you here because they did not want to deal with you anymore. At least Nathaneal follows orders for the most part. You, on the other hand, have no idea the difference between your arse hole and your mouth."

Sati wanted to say something. He was getting angry. Fred was laying it on and did not let up.

"You said you wanted us to go after the Streak," said Sati interrupting Fred.

"Did I ask you to speak? No one asked you to speak. You engage when I tell you to engage or I will ground you."

"You already grounded me," said Sati.

Fred was exasperated. The other pilots in the room were in shock that Sati was actually talking back to his wing commander.

"Sati!" Fred shouted, his patience taxed. "You need to learn discipline. You do not own that frame. You do as you are told or I swear I will ground you and you will never fly again."

"I don't want that," said Sati.

Some of the pilots laughed. Nathaneal sent to Sati and told him to shut up. Sati shut up and took the rest of the chewing out and then was ordered to sit down. He wanted Fred to let him fly again. He had gone to the infirmary and got a synth shot so that he would heal faster but it was still taking too long. The meeting let out and Nathaneal came up to Sati in the hall.

"He is going to ground you. You need to learn to shut up," said Nathaneal.

"I am already grounded. You remember, right?"

Sati was due for a physical today and if he passed that he could fly again. They ran into Faid and Blue still wearing black.

"You got yourself boinked," said Sati to Blue punching him in the arm. Blue's face lit up bright red and he turned away. Faid put his arm around Blue's waist. Someone remarked on their public display of affection. Sati had the same physiological makeup as Blue so Sati was well aware of how their joining would have to take place.

Is Parat over?" asked Nathaneal. The holiday went on for two days and there were specific things they had to do throughout the timeframe.

We have to go for the closing service, sent Faid.

It is a lot of different crap that makes Faid happy so we do it, sent Blue. Faid looked over at Blue angrily and then stormed off. Blue was not taking this seriously. Faid had not seen this side of Blue before. He though it had to do with Sati and Nathaneal. Or it could have been because Blue was a squadron lead now. Faid was the lead in this mate pair relationship and was not going to complain. He would deal with it.

Blue accompanied Nathaneal and Sati to the rec room. Nathaneal and Blue sat down in the back. Sati went to play pool with some other pilots. People were looking at Nathaneal.

They really don't like you, sent Blue.

"You missed the beat down they gave me two days ago," Nathaneal rolled up his sleeve and showed Blue the huge bruise he had on his arm from when they beat him up in the locker room.

Why don't you report that?

"It would just get worse. It is fine. I can defend myself. I am used to it."

Someone walked up to Nathaneal and kicked the chair he was in. Nathaneal stood up and so did Blue.

"Bring it to me directly," said Nathaneal to the pilot.

"We don't need your kind here."

Sati turned around holding the pool cue. Nathaneal was about to get into it.

"You want to take it outside?" said Nathaneal.

"Gladly," said the pilot and both of them teleported to the hangar.

Sati put the pool cue down, psi located Nathaneal and teleported to the hangar. Blue followed them.

Nathaneal hit the pilot. He blasted him with a psi surge and sent him across the floor. The guy recovered and came at Nathaneal. He ran up to Nathaneal and punched him in the face. The pilot punched him hard and fast. The mechanics in the hangar stopped what they were doing and circled around Nathaneal and the pilot as they battled it out. The crowd was cheering for the pilot. He was winning against Nathaneal. The pilot punched Nathaneal in the jaw and he went down. The pilot put his hands up in the air and walked in a circle in front of Nathaneal who started to get up. Nathaneal sparked up his aegis and started to wail on the pilot. He knocked him down and then got on top of him and just kept punching him. It was no contest. Nathaneal stood up. Three mechanics ran at Nathaneal and two of them held his arms and another one just started punching him in the stomach. Another mechanic handed the person punching him a wrench and he whacked Nathaneal across the chest with it and he knocked the wind out of him. The two holding him dropped him on the ground. The mechanic started hitting him in the stomach with the wrench. Sati came out of the crowd and grabbed the mechanic's wrist to stop him from hitting him. Two pilots held Sati back as the mechanic continued to hit Nathaneal. Blue sparked up his aegis and froze the whole group in place and then walked in and tried to wake Nathaneal up. Nathaneal opened his eyes and Blue helped him up still holding the crowd at bay. It was difficult for Blue to hold all those people. They were trying to shake his control.

"Just drop it," said Nathaneal getting back on his feet. "Release them." Nathaneal wiped the blood from his mouth on his sleeve. Blue released the crowd. Someone came in and tackled Blue from behind. They were still holding Sati. The mechanic with the wrench swung at Nathaneal again hitting him in the shoulder. Nathaneal put his hand up to his shoulder. Nathaneal turned and the mechanic hit him in the face with the wrench and he went down unconscious.

Fred came up to the crowd, called the group off and leaned in to help Nathaneal.

"Friggin' Jannai," the mechanic said and dropped the wrench on the ground and walked away. The crowd released Blue and Sati and went back to their work. Fred bent down and tapped Nathaneal on the shoulder to try to get him to wake up. He didn't. He was down. Fred called over an officer and had him come help him get Nathaneal up. The officer helped Fred carry Nathaneal to the side of the hangar and they sat him down against the wall. Sati and Blue came over to them.

"Why didn't you tell me this stuff was going on?" asked Fred.

"He didn't want to report it. It would just get worse," said Sati.

Fred sent to the lead mechanic and he came over to him. Fred wanted him to know this was not okay.

"Your mechanics cannot beat up on my pilots," said Fred. The lead mechanic was a little bent out of shape for being called out. The mechanics thought the pilots were elitest.

"From what I saw, your pilot started it."

"I doubt that," said Fred.

"You doubting me?" said the mechanic lead, a little irritated.

Fred did not want to get into an altercation with the mechanic lead on his turf. That would bode badly for the rest of the squadron leads.

"Just drop it," said Fred. "If this happens again I will report your guys."

The lead mechanic went back to his work. Nathaneal started to wake up. He put his hand up to his cheek and opened his mouth. His cheek hurt. Then he put his hand to his stomach.

"Are you okay?" asked Fred.

"I don't know. He wailed on me with a wrench."

"You were supposed to report it if they gave you grief."

"I would have been reporting to you every few hours."

"It was that bad?" asked Fred.

"Now do you wonder why I had a loaded gun?" said Nathaneal standing up.

"Go to the infirmary and get yourself checked out. I want you okay to fly."

"I'll go with you. I have to get a physical anyway," said Sati chiming in.

Nathaneal got up and started walking away with his hand on his stomach with Sati. Fred put his hand on Blue's shoulder as he turned to follow them.

"I want you to report anything if they start in on you as well," said Fred.

Sure, sent Blue.

For some reason the pilots and mechanics had left Blue alone. Maybe it was just that his psi was not crazy like Sati and Nathaneal. Blue walked out of the hangar and went back to his cabin. Faid had a running tap on Blue and he knew he had been a part of the fight. When Blue came in the room Faid sparked up his aegis and turned on him.

You missed the ceremony, Faid sent angrily.

Calm down, sent Blue.

You were supposed to be with me and instead you went with them.

So?

You got into a fight. Didn't you?

Blue just remembered he was not supposed to be fighting. Faid was really angry. He advanced on Blue.

You are not supposed to fight either, sent Blue.

Faid took a step forward and grabbed Blue by the collar.

You are supposed to be the mate pair. What has gotten into you?

What is wrong with you?

"It is Parat. You are supposed to be reverential. This is the most sacred Packrat holiday there is and you defiled it!" Faid broke his vow by speaking.

Faid was really angry. He sent a psi surge at Blue that sent him into the desk. Then he raced in and put his hand up to Blue's forehead and sent a pulse at him and knocked Blue out.

Faid walked out of the room and went to the cafeteria and sat down across from Lino.

"Blue is driving me crazy!" Faid said.

"Wow, you just broke your vow," said Lino looking up at him. He was drinking a protein shake.

"I am irritated. Nathaneal and Sati are making Blue crazy. He is not acting like he was before. Something has gotten into him."

"Aren't you just upset because he is your senior?"

"No, I don't care about that. He is supposed to be the pair. He is to follow my lead."

"If I understand correctly his level was higher than yours when you were paired that makes him the lead. Isn't that why you jacked him? You swore to me you were not going to do that."

"He manipulated me into doing that," said Faid.

"You are just irritated because it is Parat and you broke your vow of silence."

Faid banged his hand down on the table and then got up and went to get some food. Parat was over. Faid had held his vow through the closing ceremony so he had actually lasted the whole holiday. He would have been really angry if Blue had made him lose it earlier. He was just mad that Blue was not taking it seriously. Faid came back to the table with some noodles that were bright yellow.

"You must be starving," said Lino as he watched Faid shovel the food into his mouth.

"I haven't eaten anything in two days," said Faid.

Blue came into the cafeteria and sat down across from Faid. Lino looked at him. He did look more official in his uniform. He had three bars on his shoulder as opposed to Faid's one.

"I am sorry that I fought," said Blue. He was using his voice more since Sati and Nathaneal had shown up and Faid noticed that.

Faid did not answer, just kept eating.

"You have to talk to me. I am your mate pair."

Faid looked up and glared at him. His anger was visible.

"I didn't know that Parat was such a big deal. I would have taken it more seriously if I had known," said Blue.

"You did know. I told you Parat was sacred," said Faid really loud. He stood up and some of the other people in the cafeteria turned to see what was going on.

"The Packrat mate pair is pissed," said a mechanic.

"Shut up!" said Faid sparking up his aegis. "I am tired of people berating the Packrats. The Jannai would still be in the

City and the Zone if the Packrats had not come in and saved your asses. We killed enough Jannai to cover your sorry arse for years."

"You have a problem with the military, Packrat?" said a pilot getting up and walking away from the table and closer to Faid.

"You Psi Faction guys need to learn some manners," said another pilot and stood up.

"Don't," said Lino putting his hand on Faid's arm but Faid didn't listen. He took a step towards the first pilot and his aegis swam around him into an energy sphere and started to keen.

"What kind of energy is that?" said one of the mechanics.

The first pilot that had started it backed off. He didn't want to go up against that type of power. Faid's aegis was unstable with the kedek infusion. Faid put his hands out palms up and raised his level and it started to spark around the energy sphere.

"Stop it," said Blue standing up and sparking up his own aegis and turning on Faid.

"What are you going to do?" said Faid looking at Blue angrily.

"I am going to report you," said Blue.

"You are my mate pair. I decide what you do and do not do," said Faid.

"You do not own me," said Blue.

"They are fighting and right after Parat too. The pair lead seems to have a little bit of a problem controlling his mate," said the same mechanic and started to laugh.

Faid sent a psi surge and blew up the table that the mechanic was sitting at. Pilots scrambled out of the way.

"You cannot do this Faid," said Lino and sparked up his own aegis. The pilots in the room backed away as they felt Lino's level and saw the lightening circling around his hands.

"Shit! He is the one with the 325 level," said someone in the hall. They could all feel Lino. The room started to move away from the three of them. Fred came into the cafeteria.

"What is going on?" asked Fred.

Lino sent lightening at Faid and knocked him on the floor. His aegis went out. He had started to go psi crit. He had infused the energy sphere with the full range of his power. Blue ran over to Faid and cradled his head in his lap and held his hand up towards Lino to block him. Blue would fight for Faid if he had to.

"You two need to control your temper and get your shit back together. I don't know what happened to you two since you have been paired but it is disruptive to everyone. Just get it in gear," said Lino.

Lino waved his hands and put out his aegis. Faid came to and glared at Lino. Blue looked down at Faid and put his hand up to his cheek.

"I am sorry, I should have taken Parat more seriously and listened to you," said Blue. Faid put his hand on Blue's arm and sat up.

"All of you need to learn some discipline," Fred said to the entire hall and turned around pointing out into the crowd. "We cannot have barn yard fights in the cafeteria. What is wrong with you? Are you children?"

"That one is a Packrat terrorist. He can't help it," said someone in the hall.

Faid put his hands up. Fred shook his head. There would be no more fighting right now.

"Lino, you are grounded," said Fred.

"Why me?"

"It was your codess I saw. You used your power against a fellow soldier. That is against the rules. Take him into custody," said Fred to the MP who was against the wall. He came over and put cuffs on Lino and led him to the detention block. Fred wanted them to forget that it was Lino with the 325 level. The pilots were not supposed to know that. Lino, as an Isshin pilot was an elite position. He should have known better. Fred was going to make an example out of Lino. The Jannai were not to be given special treatment just because they were elite pilots. Nathaneal and Sati came into the cafeteria. Nathaneal had a bandage on the side of his face close to his eye where the mechanic had hit him in the head with the wrench.

"What did we miss?" asked Sati. He had just been cleared to fly and had passed his physical. It had been strenuous for him. He had tried really hard because he didn't want to be grounded any more. He had been breathing hard when he finished the treadmill portion of the physical and it had taken a toll on his body because he was not totally healed yet.

Lino was grounded and in detention for a week. Fred was taking it seriously and had made sure in each ops meeting in the Ready Room each day that he announced Lino was still grounded. Sati had been up every day with Nathaneal in the fray with the Atlantea Federation. They had been fighting the full resources of the Dionysis Air Fortress. The Dionysis had released a kedek warhead and taken out six entire squadrons from one of the Pacific Territories' battleships. It was in retaliation for blowing up one of the Atlantea Federation cruisers.

Gailen and the commanders did not want the Dionysis releasing any more warheads. One of the reasons they had given Lino the time in detention was that they wanted him to review the schematics for the Dionysis. They wanted him and Nathaneal to go in on separate missions and they needed Lino to get a better feel for the fortress.

Gailen had briefed the commanders about the mission that Lino had gone on before. The virus that he had been given had taken out multiple locations in the Atlantea Federation homeland and they had been able to maintain a strategic advantage but it had not taken out the Dionysis. That system was on a different feed it seemed. They needed Lino to figure out where that feed was. Lino had been reading plans and schematics for days. He had three tablets and many large maps all over the floor in the detention cell. Gailen came in with one of the science officers.

"We think we found a way to infiltrate the Dionysis and blow it up," said the science officer. He had a holo projector in his hand and turned it on and put it in his palm. The hologram appeared above the handheld. Lino got up from the cot in the detention cell and came up to the bars and looked at the hologram.

"There is an air shaft that flows through the entire conduit system that handles the intake exhaust from the kedek engines. If we can get a blast up there we can blow up the Dionysis."

Lino went back to the cot and picked up one of the tablets off the floor. He sifted through pages and came to a drawing of the engine intake system for the Dionysis.

"Where did you get all this from?" asked Lino coming back over to the bars.

"It was from Nathaneal's infiltration. He got a lot of good data."

"I think I read that the main air shaft is linked to the kedek reactor directly. It channels through the intake sytem so it comes directly out of the bottom of the fortress."

"You would have to get through the shields and fire a missle directly up through the shaft. It would have to be a direct hit in order for it to take."

"I know that I can teleport out of the shields but I did not send myself in," said Lino.

"We would probably need some assistance getting through the shields. We can probably disrupt the shields for a while and send a frame through," said the science officer. He pulled up another view on the hologram.

"Sati could fly both you and Nathaneal in but we would have to use a double frame unit so that we only need to get one machine in there then two can come out," said Gailen. It was just one of the solutions they were milling over.

"I want Nathaneal on the inside there is more information we need about the Atlantea Federation fleet. If he can download the schema file for the Dionysis we may be able to put their strategic advantage to rest."

THE QUADRION ISSHIN, A 9TH GENERATION MOBILE FRAME MODEL IN FRAME MODE

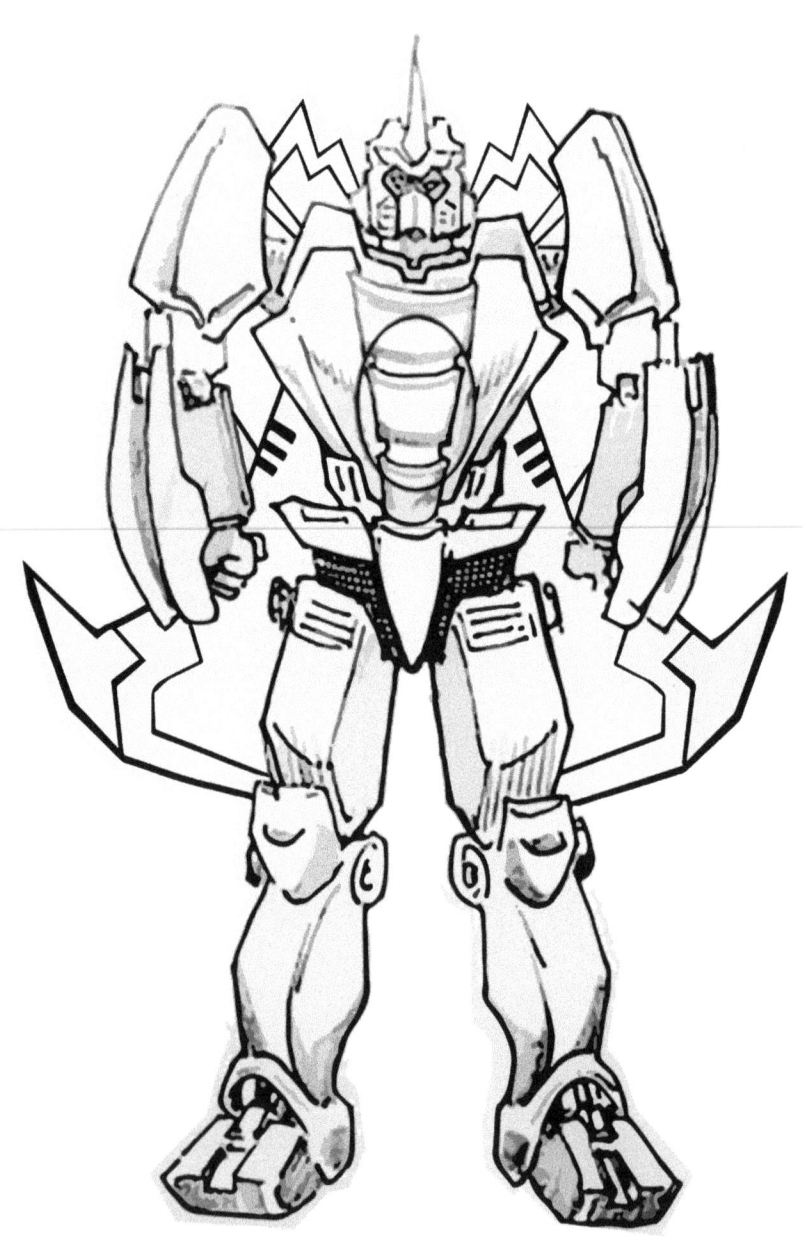

Chapter 6

Sati was in the Rec Room with Nathaneal sitting in the lounge chairs. Someone came up behind him and whacked him on the head. Sati stood up, turned around, suddenly came to attention and saluted. It was his older brother Sato Ima. He had a military cap under his arm.

"Take the optical sensor off. You look like an idiot," said Sato.

Sati scrambled and put his hand up to the side of his head and removed the optical sensor from his jack and put it in his pocket. Sato was an Isshin pilot and a squadron lead. He had gone to officer's school and was renowned for his prowess. Sati was always flying trying to reach his brother's skill level.

"When did the Esset join the battle group?" asked Nathaneal from his seat.

"Just yesterday. I am here for a lead meeting," said Sato.

Sato had come over in a shuttle from the Esset. He was going to be in a meeting with Fred and the rest of the squadron leads. Blue would have to go as well. Sati was still standing at attention.

"Is that Sato Ima?" asked another pilot in the room.

"Yeah, it looks like him. Is that Sati looking all bent out of shape?"

"Don't they have the same last name, Ima?"

"You mean Sati is related to him?"

"I think they are brothers."

"That is a hard reputation to live up to."

"You said it. Sato Ima is famous for his fighting ability and his leadership skills."

"More than you can say for Sati. He is a screw up."

"Have you heard from father?" asked Sati.

Sato stood there for a while and then put his hand up to his chin and answered. "The commander is leading the entire battle group. You probably won't get a chance to see him this time around."

Sati was disappointed. It had been a while since he had seen his father the commander of the Esset. Sato reached up and pulled Sati by the ear.

"Don't go causing too many problems," said Sato and released Sati and left.

Sati sat down and sighed. He was afraid of his brother. His family was always reminding him of how much more skilled and better mannered Sato was. It always made him feel less than.

"You can't let him get to you," said Nathaneal.

The Escalon was now under the leadership of the Esset battle group. Sati's father, Saito Ima had moved the fleet into formation and they were going to go up against the Atlantea Federation fleet with the full strength of their forces. Lino had been let out of detention and was going to be infiltrating the Dionysis' shields to take down the fortress. If they could do that, then they would level the playing field. Having the Dionysis out there made it difficult for the Pacific Territories. The battleships began firing on each other as the frames were released from the carriers and the battle group.

Sati was launched off catapult one with the rest of Fred's squadron. Lino accompanied the squad until they got to their destination point and then was led by Jane and Fred. They were going to help him get through the shields. Nathaneal went off to join the battle. Sati went after the Streak again.

Jane fired the gennen rifle at the shields and Fred moved his frame in close. As the shield visibly vibrated at the hit, Fred put the arms of the frame through the shield and opened a hole. Jane moved her frame along side Fred's and enlarged the hole. They expanded it so that Lino could get his frame in.

"You are on your own," came Fred over the comm and released the hold on the shields. Jane and Fred went back to the fighting.

Lino maneuvered to the bottom of the Dionysis and took out the missile launcher that they had loaded onto the frame. There was on missile loaded. It had been equipped with special technology. Lino leveled the missile launcher at the shaft at the bottom of the Dionysis air fortress and hovered there. Lino had to make sure that the missile went straight up the shaft. He fired the missile and then teleported the frame out of the shields. The Pacific Territories' frames pulled back from the Dionysis but continued to fight.

Suddenly, the Dionysis exploded in the sky. Sati caught the Streak out of the corner of his eye and went after it. It was advancing on the Esset and it had its blaster drawn. Saito Ima, the commander could see the Jannai frame clearly through the command center. The blaster was aimed right at them. It would be over if the command structure was compromised for the fleet. Sati came ramming up on the Streak frame and knocked it out of position. It fired and the shot missed the command center of the Esset. Sati had out his sword module and started hacking away at the Streak frame. You could see the fight through the command center window.

"Who is that?" said one of the officers.

The radar officer pinged the frame and it came back with Sati Ima's name as the pilot and the IFF response.

"It is Sati Ima from the Escalon," said the radar officer.

Commander Ima nodded as they watched the two frames battle it out. The Streak fired its guns and hit Sati's frame in the cockpit. He felt a sharp pain in his thigh. Sati's frame swiped the sword through the center of the Streak's cockpit. His machine hacked the Streak in half and the frame blew up.

"He saved the command structure of the fleet," said another officer.

Sati's frame hovered in front of the Esset for some time and then flew off.

The Atlantea Federation fleet pulled back. The Pacific Territories had won their battle today. The frames were recalled.

The rope system lowered Lino to the deck. Some of the other pilots were cheering as he came out of his frame. They had all seen the Dionysis explode in the sky. Someone put his hand on Lino's shoulder. He was smiling.

"Nice shooting," came the pilot.

Lino didn't say anything. Nathaneal came and rifled his hair. Sati came over. He had his helmet in his hand over his thigh and was leaning over slightly.

"Was that you who blew the Dionysis out of the sky?" asked Sati putting his hand out to Lino who shook his hand. "Nice job," Sati limped away and went to the infirmary.

Sati sat on the medical table. The doctor cut a hole in his flight suit at his thigh and could clearly see a nick from a bullet. He sprayed the area with the pain salve and took the retractor and checked the wound. Sati stuck out his tounge as the doctor pulled some debris out of the wound. The doctor covered the wound with a bandage and made him stay there for a while to make sure his body did not go into shock.

"Can you give me a synth shot?" asked Sati.

"We probably shouldn't. You have been in here a lot recently," said the doctor. "Let me take a reading of your immune response."

The doctor took a handheld and scanned Sati. His immune response was low. It was probably due to the amount of damage that was done by the nanomachines when he had done the machine synch.

"Yes, we should probably give you the synth. Your immune response is low. Have you been on synch supplements before?" asked the doctor.

"No, why do I need them?"

"Your body seems to think it has been compromised. I think you need to take it easy for a while. The machine synch is very hard on the body. You need to be careful."

Sati took the synth shot and went back to his room and went to sleep. The last synch he had done when he had taken off the limiter had been really harsh to him physically and he was still not completely healed from before.

Nathaneal came into the room and turned out the light. It had been a long day.

A month passed since Sati destroyed the Streak frame and saved the Esset. The command structure had wanted to recognize Lino and Sati for their contributions to the fleet, Lino for destroying the Dionysis and Sati for saving the Esset.

They were in their dress uniforms and had taken a helicopter over to the Esset. Fred came with the squadron and Jane. They were in a room with officers. It was a small room with a red floor and bookshelves. There was a desk in the center of the room. Officers were standing at the corners. Sati's brother was there as well. Fred stood with Jane and Nathaneal at the side behind Lino and Sati. The two of them stood in a tight row in front of Sati's father and another officer. Sati's father Saito was a stern and serious man. He had a harsh face and was tall and thin. The commander called Lino and he took a step forward.

"For your valor and courageous service in the destruction of the Dionysis, I award you the Commendation of the Nebula," said Sati's father and pinned the medal to Lino's chest. Commander Ima turned towards Sati and took the medal out of the box.

"For your fighting prowess in saving the Esset, I award you the Commendation of the Phoenix." Sati's father pinned the medal on Sati's chest and Sati saluted and stepped back in line.

Sati's father reached out to shake Lino's hand. Commander Ima put his hand on Sati's shoulder and led him out of the room. They walked down the hall to his father's office and went inside. His father sat down behind the desk and took off his cap and sat in front of him. He opened the drawer in the desk and took out a cigar from a box. Sati stood at attention.

"You can relax," said Saito. Sati remained at attention.

Sati's father clipped the end of the cigar with the cutter, then lit it and looked at it.

"You have been having trouble?" asked Saito.

"No sir," said Sati.

"I heard you went off half-cocked and engaged before you were ordered."

Sati opened his mouth to speak but was silenced by his father.

"I also heard they had to take the limiter settings off your frame because you did something stupid."

"I wanted to make sure that we killed the enemy, sir," said Sati.

"I hear you got your frame busted up pretty good as well. They had to replace the arm and bang the bullet holes out of it."

His father took a puff of the cigar, then got up and came to stand in front of Sati. He leaned against the desk.

"I hear you got in a fight in the hangar."

How did his father know all this.

"We separated you and Nathaneal for this same type of behavior before. Do you want me to do that again?"

"No sir, it was difficult to be away from Nathaneal."

"Did you celebrate Parat?" asked Sati's father.

"No sir, I did not."

"You should be reverential to your mate pair. We let you get mate paired even through we thought better of it, your mother and I. We didn't want you to depend on your codess so much but it seems that you depend on it for your frame navigation. Why don't you just fly like the rest of the pilots?"

"I want to be the best pilot I can be. That requires me to use my codess, sir."

"That was the answer I expected from you. Do you want the limiter setting put back on the frame?"

"Yes sir, that would be helpful, sir. The battle determines if turning off the limiter is required or not."

"I hear the frame you destroyed with the Streak?"

"Yes sir."

"The Streak shot you down before didn't it?"

"Yes sir."

"Be careful with the limiter."

"Yes sir."

Sati's father went back to the desk and took a set of bars off the table and then moved over to Sati and put the bar on his shoulder patch over the three bars that were already there.

"You are dismissed."

"Yes sir, thank you sir," said Sati, stuck out his foot, turned around and walked out of the room.

Sati leaned against the wall in the hallway. He sighed. His father was very official. He meant what he said. Giving Sati a boost in rank was his way of showing his support for Sati who went back to the original room they were in. Fred saw Sati come back in and moved over to him. Sati's brother slapped him on the arm. Sato took Sati by the neck and forced him to lean over, whacking him on the head.

"Stop it," said Sati standing up and moving away from Sato who was taller than Sati. Actually they looked very similar. Sato's hair was shorter and darker.

"He shows you his love by making you a lieutenant?" asked Sato.

"Symbolically only," said Fred coming up to him. The bar that Sati's father had put on his shoulder was silver and not gold. It didn't mean much. It was not an official boost in rank.

"I am not an officer. I cannot be a lieutenant," said Sati. Unlike Sato who had gone to the military academy, Sati had been given a choice out of the Psi Faction. Go to the military or remain a test subject. They had conscripted him directly into a Quadrion fighter group with Nathaneal. Sati had wanted to fly and that is why he went. Nathaneal just went with him because he didn't want to be alone and didn't want to stay at the Psi Faction. They had received flight training together and that is when they started to think about becoming mate pairs.

Sati had brought up the idea of getting mate paired to his mother. She had refused. He then became suicidal and reckless, flying like a crazy person, not caring about his well being or safety. His father stepped in and had him committed to the military hospital. They determined that they had to allow him to be paired or it would be determinetal to his sanity. His dangerous flying is what got him shot down by the Streak. He had buzzed the Streak and the Jannai pilot had not appreciated that and went after him for the kill. It was lucky that Sati had actually survived. The Streak had shot his plane up and it was on fire when he crashed into the ocean.

Sati's father had always been worried about him, even when he was at the Psi Faction. Like Blue, Sati had come in as a child. Not as young as Blue, but they had placed him there when they found his psi potential was high. Sati was a citizen like Lino. Sati's father had wanted both of his children to have the best chance that they could in life. A career in the military was a way to make that happen. Sati's father had encouraged him to be a pilot.

When they finally let Sati be mate paired with Nathaneal, Sati's father and mother had come to the ceremony. It had been very emotional for them to see their child affected by the visible manifestation of codess. They had initially not know that Sati had been operated on to make him gender neutral. It had been a shock to his mother that first time after the operation to see her child miraculously transformed. It had taken some doing to get that through his mother's head. Sati had a difficult time with accepting it initially since he was older than Blue when it happened. He had becom suicidal then. They had to have him treated then to ensure he had a proper understanding of himself and his gender. Nathaneal had helped him through it. That was one of the reasons Sati wanted to be mate paired to Nathaneal because Nathaneal knew everything about him.

Sati and Nathaneal had been in the same squadron when they had transferred out of flight school and Sati had joined the Essex carrier group. The Streak shot him down while he was at the Essex. After he had been committed he had returned back to the Essex. Then he was mate paired offshore at one of the stations in the Pacific Islands. He started getting into fights with the crew and the mechanics. He had become more aggressive because they had not consummated their mate pair relationship. They finally did and the fighting died down but the damage was already done. They separated them and Sati was transferred to the Erez. It was only with the recent escalation of the fighting that they had considered bringing Sati and Nathaneal back to the same ship. Sati's father had Sati transferred back. He wanted him closer and having the Escalon join the Esset fleet made it so that he could keep an eye on Sati. With all the fighting Commander Ima didn't want Sati to go crazy again.

Fred looked at his watch and signaled the team. It was time to go back to the Escalon.

"See you up there," said Sato and punched Sati in the arm, walking off.

Fred and his team were taxied back to the Escalon in the same helecopter that brought them over.

Sati and Nathaneal went back to their room.

"I think you look more official now," said Nathaneal

touching the medal at Sati's chest. "You really saved the day. The Streak could have killed your father."

Sati took off the medal and chucked it on the desk.

"It is just a piece of metal. It doesn't mean anything," said Sati.

"What is your problem Sati? You earned that." asked Nathaneal.

"Why doesn't he just say he loves me? He doesn't need to give me some stripes and a medal."

"You know that about him Sati, This has happened before. Don't get depressed about it."

"I am depressed. I just want him to say that he loves me. I still think he is hurt that I am not the way I was before."

"Don't start in on that again," said Nathaneal coming up to Sati and putting his hands around his waist. Sati tried to push him off.

"I want him to acknowledge me for who I am now. I am still the same person," said Sati.

"We have gone through this before Sati. You are not the same person. Your whole identity is different," said Nathaneal.

"But why can't he accept that? Why can't he say he loves me? My mother won't even accept it..." Sati trailed off and opened the desk drawer and pulled out a letter from his mother. He put the letter at Nathaneal's chest and continued.

"She can't say she loves me either. She just talks about herself and when she used to go shopping with me as a child. She even says something about pretty dresses in there. She doesn't accept me either," said Sati exasperated. He was waving his arms and his aegis was sparking around his hands.

"Calm down Sati."

"No, they never accepted me. My mother told me she didn't want any of them in her family. Them! Like being the way I am now is something bad. I can't stand them. I wish I were like Sato."

"Are we going to go through this again, Sati? Are you going to get all bent out of shape and start flying like a maniac again? Do I have to tell Fred? They will put you on notice. It is too close since the last time this happened. They remember. That is why your father called you in after giving you the medal. You know that right?"

"He knew about the fight in the hangar. Is he keeping tabs on me? Why would he even want to know that? I am irrelevant to them. Even my mother can't call me by my name on the phone. She won't even acknowledge me. The last time she called me, she called it. She called me an it, Nathaneal." Sati was screaming.

Someone knocked on the door. Nathaneal went to open it.

"Is something wrong in here?" asked the officer. Sati put his hand behind his back.

"No sir, we were just having a discussion," said Nathaneal.

"Keep it down then," said the officer and turned and walked away.

Sati slammed the door behind the officer and his aegis sparked out of control.

"Sati, you need to be reasonable," said Nathaneal.

"I am not reasonable Nathaneal. I am insane. You know that. They declared that at the hearing when they committed me."

"Sati, you take your medication on time every day and you are just fine."

Sati looked down at his hands. He tried to put out the aegis but couldn't. His aegis was glowing blue and orange. He shook his hands.

"No, they said that I am schizophrenic and I have to be cleared to fly every month. What type of pilot needs that? One that is sane? No Nathaneal, they screwed me in the head, then they screwed with my body and they made it so my parents won't even see me for who I am."

"Then it is time to go to the doctor Sati and tell them what is going on."

"I am not going to do that. They will ground me," said Sati and shook his hands again. He looked concerned. Sati's aegis was blue when he was controlled. But if he went crazy it glowed orange. His aegis was mostly blue now but there were sparks of orange around his hands.

"Is it starting?"

Sati put his hands down to his sides, sucked in a breath and tried hard to put his aegis out. It continued sparking and then died out. It had taken a lot of his control.

"It is coming. I can feel it," said Sati.

"Was it the Streak? That was a brutal fight the way that pilot beat up your frame?"

Sati walked towards Nathaneal and came up to him and hugged him. He buried his face into Nathaneal's chest and hugged him tighter.

"Don't leave me when I go crazy, Nathaneal, don't leave me alone."

"I haven't done it before and I won't do it now. How much time do we have before it happens again?"

"It could be any day now."

"How long have you known Sati? You should have told me."

"I thought I could handle it. I thought this time it would be different. It has been going on for a week, I get trapped by racing thoughts and am scared all the time. I am scared on the ground. I keep seeing the Streak when I go up. I am seeing things."

"Maybe Raven can heal you," responded Nathaneal.

"It is worth a try. Lets go see if we can find him," said Sati.

They walked out of the cabin holding hands. Someone remarked on it as they walked through the hall. Nathaneal was pulling Sati behind him. Nathaneal was the mate pair lead. His level was technically the same as Sati's but his aegis was stable unlike Sati's so when they were paired the Prophets that had paired them gave Nathaneal the position.

They went into the cafeteria. Sati pulled his hand away from Nathaneal the minute they entered. Raven was sitting with Blue and Lino. Nathaneal and Sati walked over and sat down.

Blue looked up at Sati. He could feel him. "Are you alright? I've felt this before," said Blue to Sati. He stopped eating and looked concerned. He could feel something off about Sati. It was like his energy was unstable and his emotions.

Sati looked around the room. He looked scared. He moved slightly closer to Nathaneal, put his hand up to his mouth and stared out into the cafeteria.

"Sati is a little scared right now," said Nathaneal.

Sati nodded but did not look at them. He didn't want to meet their eyes. They could steal his soul if he met their eyes.

"Can you heal him?" Nathaneal asked Raven.

"I can try. What is wrong?"

"He has a mental thing."

Sati turned back around and looked at the ceiling and spoke, "Sati is crazy." He put his arm out on the table with his palm down. Raven put his hand on Sati's arm. Sati looked out into the crowd. He was afraid. Raven held his arm for a while and then his eyes opened wide and he looked over at Sati.

"You are schizophrenic?" asked Raven taking his hand off Sati's arm.

Lino looked over at Sati.

"How can he fly then?" asked Lino.

"He gets cleared every month and takes medication," said Nathaneal. "If he does not pass the mental exam he gets grounded."

Sati nodded and began to bite his nails. Raven started to infuse healing energy into Sati's arm. He had to get the source identified first before he could start healing him. He didn't know if he could fix that. It wasn't like his mind was technically hurt. The chemical composition was just different. Sati's mind was very convoluted. Raven could see some scary images in Sati's mind and he pulled his hand away.

"Are you really seeing such frightening things right now?" asked Raven.

Sati nodded. He was terrified. He took his hand out of his mouth and put it on top of Nathaneal's under the table and held on for dear life. Raven put his hand back on Sati's arm and tried again. He tried for some time but there was nothing he could do. Sati's mental stability was too far gone.

"I can't heal him. If you had come to me sooner I might have been able to do something," said Raven.

"It was worth a shot," said Nathaneal.

Sati stood up and looked out into the cafeteria and screamed at the top of his lungs, "you need to be careful of the Jannai. They are coming to get us all!"

The crowd just laughed at him. They thought it was a joke. Sati sat back down.

"Is he okay to fly?" asked Lino.

"He flys until they ground him," said Nathaneal. "That is how it has always been. It is on his record to check. He has a scheduled check in two days."

The alarm came over the intercom. "Condition Red all pilots to your aircraft. Condition Red." All the pilots in the cafeteria got up and started moving towards the door. Sati did not get up. Nathaneal had to tap him on the shoulder and get him to come.

"That is dangerous for him to fly in his condition," said Blue. "I am going to report him."

"Don't do that Julian, he needs to fly. That is the only place where he feels safe. Don't take that away from him. He needs that right now."

They walked to the locker room and suited up.

Sati passed his mental exam but just barely. He was hallucinating when he was taking the exam. They asked him 30 questions and he had to answer off the top of his head. He missed a few but his score was high enough to pass him.

He suited up and went to the Ready Room. The rest of the squadrons and leads were already there. Sati walked up to the front of the room and handed Fred the piece of paper with his score on it.

"Good, you are okay to fly," said Fred. He gave Sati some time to go back and sit next to Nathaneal. A pilot in the room spoke up as Sati walked by him.

"Freak," the pilot coughed out.

Sati sparked up his aegis and pointed his finger at the pilot and then put it out. His aegis was clearly glowing orange now. Nathaneal saw that and had no idea how Sati had passed his mental exam. Fred started the briefing. Then suddenly Sati picked up a sending. It was from the Jannai.

Send the yellow Isshin pilot, come.

Sati looked at Nathaneal. It was the Jannai Streak pilot. He was not dead. The sending was the same. Sati got scared. He put his hand on Nathaneal's knee and started to squeeze it.

It is okay, Nathaneal sent to Sati.

He is going to kill me, sent Sati and put his hand up to his mouth. He had cut the fingers out of his gloves. He held his helmet tightly with the other hand. Sati turned to face Nathaneal and moved to the edge of the seat. Sati started to get up. Nathaneal put his hand on his shoulder and held him in place.

Don't, he will ground you, sent Nathaneal. Sati looked over at him with his fingers in his mouth.

Fred dismissed the pilots and everyone went to the hangar. Sati got up on the rope system and climbed into the cockpit. He closed the cockpit door. He put his hand on the main instrument panel and touched it.

"You are going to be good to me today, right Isshin?" asked Sati. "We need to get the Streak pilot before he gets us."

Sati released his jack and it connected to the port. He put on the helmet and initiated the start up procedure. He sent to Nathaneal.

I am scared.

Just do like you always do. You are a good pilot.

The Jannai are going to skin me alive if I get caught. They are going to take out my eyeballs, sent Sati.

Just fly like you know how. Do not turn off the limiter, sent Nathaneal. He was really concerned for Sati who had flown before in this state but Nathaneal had never seen him fly with his aegis completely orange. He knew this could end badly.

One by one the frames launched off the catapult. When it came time for Sati's launch he had to give acknowledgement.

"Sati Ima, Ishhin F22-12 launching!" The catapult went off and it threw the frame into the air. He transformed into aircraft mode. Nathaneal came over his radio.

"Stay in aircraft mode. Do not engage. Do not fly out of formation."

Fred heard the conversation over the comm and wondered for a moment if he should have grounded Sati.

"Sati, are you okay?" came Fred.

"Yes sir, Sati is cleared and ready."

"Good," said Fred and the frames got into formation.

They had to fly a good distance to the sortie point. They were the cover for another squadron escorting the science vessel Poseidon.

Suddenly the Streak pilot came out of nowhere and started shooting at Sati's frame. It was engaging him alone. It flew by the squadron and then banked and turned, arming a missle. The Streak had him locked on.

"Permission to engage?" asked Sati. The alarm in Sati's cockpit was on.

"Do not fire until fired upon," came the tower.

"Then I'm gone!"

"Sati wait," called Fred but Sati was already gone. He veered off and transfored and stopped his trajectory, then transformed back to aircraft mode and went after the Streak. It blew by them.

"He is not okay to fly is he, Nathaneal?" asked Fred.

"Permission to support?" asked Nathaneal.

"Denied." Nathaneal stayed in formation.

The Streak took Sati way out of the sortie point and into the mountains. He was letting Sati chase him. Sati was on him tight. The Streak was flying recklessly. Sati was breathing hard. He was seeing other planes around him. He was hallucinating.

"Hold it together, Sati," he said to himself and flew off out of the mountains. It was too much.

"F22-12 you are out too far," came the tower. The Streak left the island mountains and transformed and changed direction and went after Sati who turned around and went back. He climbed higher into the sky. He could see planes on him now and they were firing. The Streak came in and fired guns at Sati's plane and hit it in the engine. The engine started to flame out.

"Engine one is out. Shutting it down," Sati pulled his hand out of the stirrup control and pushed the switch to disengage the engine. The second engine took up the slack and kept the plane level.

Sati picked up a sending from the Jannai.

You are dead.

The Streak transformed. Sati transformed right along with it and they started going at each other with the sword modules. The Streak was playing for keeps. It hacked up Sati's frame. Sati was completely defensive.

"Permission to support?" asked Nathaneal again. They could see the Streak battling with Sati. There were five other frames that had joined the fight. It was the only battle in the area. Sati was completely defensive.

"Denied," said Fred.. "Tower we have a defensive pilot. Permission to engage."

"Your squadron is running cover for Poseidon. Permission denied," came the tower.

"Come on!" cried Lino. "There is no way he can get himself out of that."

Sati transformed and ran. He was surrounded by Jannai. He was terrified. The Streak and the five other Jannai frames were completely overwhelming him as he was holding his own.

"Engaging!' Nathaneal veered off and left formation and went to help Sati.

"Nathaneal get back in formation!" yelled Fred.

"I can't hear you sir there is something wrong with my radio," said Nathaneal and then turned off the comm.

"F22-11 has disengaged communication line. Please acknowledge?" came the tower.

"Dejarre do not leave formation," ordered Fred.

"Come on, that is a slaughter," said Lino. From where they were they could see the six frames on Sati furiously attacking his frame.

"Do not leave formation," repeated Fred.

Sati transformed and ran. The Streak went after him. The alarm came on in his cockpit. The Streak has missile lock. Sati started teleporting the frame wildly. Nathaneal could see the desperation in his tactics. The other six frames transformed and went after him. The Streak had chopped the leg off Sati's frame.

Nathaneal blew up one of the frames on Sati and went in for the kill on another one. Two frames disengaged and went after Nathaneal who flew off and they went after him. He wanted to get them away from Sati. The Streak fired the guns and hit Sati's frame again. An alarm came on in the cockpit. Sati pulled the limiter screen and the keyboard down and turned off the limiter and pushed the control. Sati still had three frames and the Streak on him. He put his hands back through the stirrup controls and sparked up his aegis. His eyes lit up and the aegis sparked around his hands. It was completely orange. He was delusional. Sati teleported the frame and reversed direction, transforming almost on top of the Streak and rammed into it. The Streak transformed and Sati hacked the arms off the frame. The Streak turned and ran. Nathaneal destroyed the other two frames and came back to Sati and blew past him and went after the Streak.

Sati attacked one of the three frames that were on him and blew it up. Then he teleported over to the other two and blew them up in succession with the gennen rifle. There was just the Streak now.

Nathaneal turned his comm line back on and could hear Sati calling to him.

"Go back to formation," said Sati repeating it over and over.

"No, I'll stay and protect you."

"You can't protect me right now. Go back to formation."

Nathaneal went back to formation. Fred and his squadron were returning to base.

"You are grounded," came Fred as Nathaneal got back into formation.

Their mission was over the Poseidon had reached its target.

"Are you just going to leave him out there?" asked Nathaneal.

Sati joined the formation again. His plane was on fire. The plane was wobbling as he tried to keep in line.

"Sati..." said Fred who was interrupted by an explosion. Sati's frame started to slow down. The smoke trail got larger. Sati tapped the main panel. There were multiple error messages on the screen. Sati was falling out of formation.

"Keep it tight," said Fred. Sati was pulling back on the stirrup controls to try to bring the plane back up into formation. He started speeding up.

"Stay in formation, Sati," yelled Fred over the comm.

"I can't," he was fighting the controls. Nathaneal could see flames coming out of the back of Sati's frame.

The alarm came on again in the cockpit.

"He's on fire," said Nathaneal.

Sati sped up and blew past the formation.

"Permission to land, F22-12?" requested Sati. They could see the Esclaon up ahead. His plane was faltering in the sky and the error message read 'Critical Error.'

"Permission to land," Sati repeated. The fire grew.

"Permission granted," came the tower.

Sati came in on approach. An explosion could be heard in the engine. The engine started to flame out. Sati was approaching too fast.

"Need the net," said Sati.

The net started to deploy on the deck. Sati's plane was coming in wild.

"You are too low," came the cat officer.

Sati's plane was wobbling in the air. The whole back of the frame was on fire. The engine flamed out and Sati's frame came hurtling in. He pulled the nose up. The wheels touched down and then collapsed and the plane came scraping across the deck and was caught by the net. Sati opened the cockpit and scrambled out of the frame and fell against the deck. The deck crew came running up to him, as did the fire crew and started trying to put out the fire. Someone came over to Sati and asked him if he were okay. Sati backed up from him and started to walk away.

"We need to check you out, sir," said the crewmember.

"No," said Sati and took a step back. He pulled off his helmet and started looking around for Nathaneal.

Nathaneal landed with the rest of the formation in frame mode and the frames were moved to the hangar. Nathaneal ran out of the hangar and started to climb the stairs to go to the deck.

Sati was still roaming around on the deck. There was a medical officer following him. Nathaneal walked up to him. The medical officer called out to Nathaneal.

"We need to get him checked out."

"Sati come with me," said Nathaneal.

"No, the Streak is coming."

"The Streak is not here Sati. You are back on deck. You are okay."

"It is coming for me," said Sati dropping the helmet on the deck. He was walking around in circles.

There were burn marks on his flight suit on one side and a hole in the back.

"Sati do you hurt anywhere?" asked Nathaneal looking at the back of his flight suit. Nathaneal looked over at the frame. It was shot up pretty bad. There were bullet holes all throughout the fuselage and the leg was missing. The bottom of the frame was still sparking, but they had put out the fire.

Sati stopped walking around and put his hand on his side. It did hurt him. He pulled his hand away and it was red with blood. He looked down at his hand and then held it up to Nathaneal.

"Sati come with me now," said Nathaneal.

Fred came out onto the deck and walked up to them. The medical officer was still following them around. Sati would not stop walking in circles.

"Sati!" said Fred. Sati sparked up his aegis and put his hands up to his head. Nathaneal shook his head and spoke to Fred.

"He's not really here right now," said Nathaneal.

Fred looked over at the state of the plane and was shocked. How had he even managed to land with all the damage. His frame was pretty much a total loss.

"Sati?" called Fred.

Sati looked over at him and then walked up to him and started talking. "The Streak is coming to kill us all." Sati backed up from Nathaneal and then ran below deck.

"Sir?" Nathaneal saluted waiting.

"Go after him," said Fred.

Fred walked up to the frame and put his hand on the nose. The fire had been put out. The left wing was hacked to pieces and the right wing was missing. Fred had no idea how he had managed to land the plane. There were bullet holes throughout the frame and the right engine was destroyed. There was a crack at the back and there was a large gash right behind the cockpit. The Streak had almost cut the frame in half. Fred went back to the hangar. He was going to have to start negotiations to get another frame for his pilot. That would not be an easy sell to get another Isshin.

Sati blew past a group of pilots in the hall and actually knocked one down.

"Hey, crazy ass!" the pilot called out to Sati but he did not respond just kept running.

"Sorry," said Nathaneal as he ran by.

Sati ran to the locker room. He opened the locked and pulled out a gun and pointed it out into the room. He was alone in the locker room fortunately.

"Sati?" Nathaneal said and put his hands up so that Sati could see he wasn't a threat.

"The Streak is coming to get me," said Sati walking around in circles with the gun out.

A few people came into the locker room. Nathaneal waved them out.

"Sati you need to come with me you are wounded," said Nathaneal.

"No, the Streak is coming for me. I have to protect myself."

Fred came into the locker room.

"Back off sir," said Nathaneal. "He doesn't know what he is doing right now."

"Sati," called Fred.

Sati whirled on him and pointed the gun at him.

"You keep the Streak away from me," said Sati cocking the gun. He took a step towards Fred.

The military police came into the locker room.

"Back off. He is afraid of you," said Nathaneal with his hand out towards Sati. He took a step forward.

Sati took the gun and put it in his mouth.

"Sati!" screamed Nathaneal. Sati pulled the gun out of his mouth and pointed it at the military police. The military police raised their guns on him. Blood had soaked the side of Sati's flight suit. Sati put his hand to his side and held it. He was in pain.

"Sati, give me the gun," said Nathaneal and put out his hand.

Fred pushed the military police back but they did not pay him any mind and advanced on Sati who backed into the lockers and leaned up hard against them. Sati put the safety back on the gun. The military police took a step forward.

"I just want the Streak to leave me alone," he said weakly. He slid down the locker and came to sit on the ground. "So that I can fly."

Sati looked up at Nathaneal, "I am in trouble, right?"

"You are safe that is all that matters. We need to take you to the doctor. You are hurt," said Nathaneal.

Sati couldn't focus on Nathaneal anymore. His vision was blurry. He started to speak again then passed out on the floor. The military police pushed Nathaneal out of the way and dragged Sati up by the arms.

"Take him to the infirmary first before you put him in hack," said Fred.

Nathaneal watched them take him.

"How did he land that plane?" asked Fred. "That frame was shot to hell."

"Sati is an excellent pilot," said Nathaneal.

"He withstood six for that long," said Fred. He couldn't believe the state of the frame. "I said that you were grounded before, but I am not going to do that to you. Why does he fly?"

"Because that is the only place he feels safe."

"How long has this been going on?"

"For over a week, sir," said Nathaneal.

"You mean I have had a crazy pilot up there for a week?"

"Yes sir."

"What happens to him?"

"He starts hallucinating and gets afraid of everything. Flying is the only thing that keeps him sane."

"I read his report but I just thought that was fighting and silly antics. I didn't know that this was real. That he really is crazy."

"Sati has been dealing with this for a while sir. They have him on medication. It just gets out of hand every now and then."

"I can't have him flying if he is hallucinating. I will have to ground him."

"You can't do that sir. He will go crazy."

"I can't have a hallucinating pilot. It would be dangerous for the other people in the squadron."

"I'll watch him."

"It is unsafe Nathaneal."

"He will be my responsibility. He is my responsibility. He is my mate pair."

"He is grounded until he gets out of the infirmary. Then we will see if he can pass another mental exam and is okay to fly."

Fred left the locker room and left Nathaneal there. Nathaneal picked up the gun and closed Sati's locker. He put the gun in his own locker and made sure the safety was on. He didn't want Sati to have another excuse to do that again. He had actually put the gun in his mouth. That told Nathaneal he was suicidal again. He could have killed himself. Nathaneal walked to the infirmary. Sati was on his back on the medical table. They had cut a hole in his flight suit. He was all bruised up from the machine synch and he had been shot. The plane had stopped most of the velocity of the bullet but it had still hit him. The military police were there as they were pulling the bullet out of him and he was cuffed to the side of the bed. The doctor pulled the bullet out with a metal instrument and dropped it in a tray. Sati woke up and put out his hand. He could see Nathaneal who moved in and took his hand.

"I messed up," said Sati.

"Yes, you did," said Nathaneal. "If you hadn't pulled a gun you might have been let off the hook."

The doctor bandaged him up.

"We are done," said the doctor.

"Get up," said the military police officer. They took the handcuffs off him.

Sati sat up and Nathaneal helped him to his feet. They escorted him out of the infirmary. Fred was standing outside. Fred stopped them as they turned past him.

"Give me your wings," said Fred and put out his hand to Sati.

"No," Sati said but he knew he couldn't do anything. He put his hands up to the pin and pulled it off his flight suit and put the pin in Fred's hand. Sati looked defeated.

"You will get these back when you pass a mental exam to my satisfaction and not before that. Take him."

Chapter 7

Sati failed three mental exams in a row. He had one more left and if he did not pass that he was grounded for the month. Fred was concerned that he was not going to have a pilot. He had started the negotiations to get a new Isshin and they had brought one over from the Esset that had been decommissioned. It needed some work. The mechanics had it now and were working on the configuration. There were also some technology upgrades that needed to occur. They had kept Sati in hack for three days and he had been hallucinating the entire time. He called out to the guards who were stationed in the room. They went outside so they could not hear him.

"He is completely crazy?" asked the one guard to the other.

"He has been like that for all my shifts so far. I don't think they are going to let him out."

Nathaneal came up to the detention block and requested to be let in.

"You probably should wait. He has been wailing in there for the past few hours."

"Wailing?" asked Nathaneal.

"He has been saying something about some Streak pilot going to shoot him out of the sky. He is insane," said the guard.

Nathaneal walked past them and went into the detention block. Sati didn't notice him as Nathaneal came up to the bars. Sati was walking around in a circle with his hands up to his head and talking to himself. Nathaneal stood there for a while and called his name but Sati did not register him. Nathaneal left and went to the cafeteria. He sat down with Faid and Blue.

"How is your mate pair?" asked Faid taking a sip of his coffee.

"Not good. He really went far away this time," said Nathaneal. "I have a running tap on him. He is trapped in the fight with the Streak right now."

Blue tapped Nathaneal and could sense what he was feeling with Sati.

"Wow, he is hallucinating that? How can he make up stuff like that?" asked Blue.

"No, that fight was real. He is reliving it."

"He went up against that?" asked Blue. He could still sense what Sati was thinking.

Suddenly the tap went silent. Something was wrong. Sati was feeling pain. Nathaneal got up. "I have to go."

"Something just happened," said Blue turing to Faid. "I think he is hurting himself."

Sati had found a piece of glass in the detention cell and started stabbing his thigh with it. He kept repeating 'bullet holes' and continued to stab himself. Nathaneal came into the detention hall again and called Sati over. He registered him this time.

"Sati, what are you doing?"

"Making bullet holes where the Streak shot me."

"You can't do that Sati. You will hurt yourself."

Sati stopped and threw the piece of glass on the floor.

"Do you want to go to the hospital Sati? They can take care of you there."

"That is a scary place. I don't want to go there," said Sati and looked up at Nathaneal. He had a far away look in his eyes.

"Sati where are you right now?"

"I am in the Isshin. We are fighting the Jannai."

"We Sati, who is we?"

"Me and the Isshin we are fighting the Jannai.

The guard came into the detention hall. Luckily the blood from the stab wounds that Sati had inflicted on himself could not be seen through his black uniform.

"Get the Jannai out of here," screamed Sati and waved at the guard.

The guard put his hand up to the side of his head and made a motion calling Sati crazy then walked out again.

"Sati?"

"Yes Nathaneal."

"You need to get a hold of yourself. You want to fly don't you?"

"Yes, I want to fly."

"You cannot fly Sati if you don't get a hold of yourself. They will ground you for a month."

"I want to fly," said Sati and came up to the bars and put his hands on them and looked at Nathaneal.

"You need to pass your mental exam today Sati. You can't do this crazy stuff anymore.

The medical technican came into the detention hall with a stool and put the stool down in front of Sati's cell.

"Are you ready for your mental exam?" asked the technician as he sat down facing Sati.

Sati thought about it for a moment and said yes.

"You need to leave," said the medical technician to Nathaneal.

"Goodluck Sati. Remember you want to fly."

"Yes, I want to fly," said Sati and sat down on the cot.

Nathaneal heard the technican start the questions as he went to leave.

"What is your name?"

"Sati Ima," came the answer.

"What is your psi level?"

"Psi levels are not supposed to be discussed. My level is 100."

"Good, what day is it?"

Sati had to think about that for a moment. He didn't know. He was going to get it wrong.

"Friday."

"No, that is wrong," said the technician. "It is Tuesday." The technician marked an 'X' on the tablet.

"Who is the Emperor?"

"Charles Dejarre. Lino is his son. He is the Viceroy. He is an Isshin pilot."

"Where are you?"

"On the Esset battleship."

"No Sati, that is wrong. You are on the Escalon." The technican marked an 'X' again. "You can get three more questions wrong Sati and then you fail for the month."

Try harder, sent Nathaneal as he walked out of the detention block. Sati looked towards the door and continued answering the questions.

Nathaneal didn't think he was going to pass. He walked back to the cafeteria. Faid and Blue were still there. They had been joined by Lino who had on his dress uniform. He had a pin on his chest and a braided rope embellishment around his shoulder. His cap was on the table.

"Why are you dressed up?" asked Nathaneal.

"A representative of the Elite Imperial Guard and the Emperor's ministers are here. I have a meeting with them shortly as the Viceroy," said Lino.

"Why would they come all the way out here?" asked Nathaneal.

"They are on the way to the Saraset Islands. The Atlantea Federation has surrendered that port and they are signing a treaty."

"You mean we won one?" asked Faid.

"Yes, the Saraset Islands are free of their occupation," said Lino.

Lino picked up a sending from Gailen and stood up and left the cafeteria.

"That was rude," said Blue.

"The ministers are on him. I don't think he really has any say in any of this. He is just a figurehead," said Faid.

Lino walked up the staircase and opened the door to the Command Center. The Captain and the crew saluted Lino who did not salute back and came to stand next to Gailen. There were a lot of people with the ministers and the Elite Imperial Guard. Lino did not know why they needed all these people. Anis was also there.

"Ameliano, you look well," said Shennen, the Captain in the Elite Imperial Guard.

"Cut to the chase," said Lino. He didn't want to be here and he had no idea why Anis would be all the way out here. Anis was dressed in full regalia.

Shennen looked at Lino. The military had made him more direct.

"We want the Escalon to go on a special mission," said a minister.

"Why are you asking me this? You need to be asking Commander Ima. I don't lead the battle fleet," said Lino.

"We already asked Commander Ima. We are asking you now."

"Then what did he say?"

"He said that the Escalon cannot leave the battle group."

"Then that is what I am saying," said Lino.

"Ameliano, be reasonable," said Shennen.

"This is the military. You need to follow the chain of command. I am nowhere near the chain of command" said Lino.

"Then we will move your Trance Channeler back to the Jannassee Islands," said the minister.

"Fine, blackmail me. Take Gloughster back to his homeland so that he can be with the Emperor," barked Lino who started to walk out of the Command Center.

"The Emperor is dead your Majesty. You are the Emperor."

"What?" Lino dropped his cap on the ground and took a step back.

Anis came out from the group and walked up to Lino and put his hand on his shoulder.

"That is why I am here. I cannot authorize anything. You have to as the Emperor. I will go to the Jannassee Islands," said Anis.

"No, this is crazy. I am not the Emperor."

A voice came from behind Lino, "yes, you are."

Lino spun around. It was Gloughster. He was dressed like Justine had been when Lino first met her with the cape with the headdress and the pointed rings. Lino was glad to see Gloughster. He had missed him.

"Your psi level has been raised," said Lino. Gloughster seemed to float over the floor towards him.

"It was my duty as the Emperor's Trance Channeler," said Gloughster.

"Why is my father dead?" Lino didn't understand.

"He was assassinated," said Shennen. "We are your Elite Imperial Guard now." Shennen hesitated then continued. "Order the Escalon to go on this mission your Majesty. The fleet is yours."

"Where is Saya?" asked Lino.

"She is here as my Adept," said Gloughster. "She is below deck."

"I am not going anywhere," said Lino.

"I will go to the Jannassee Islands," said Anis. "But you need to authorize it."

"You need to do this your Majesty," said Shennen.

Lino took Gloughster by the hand and vanished. He materialized with Gloughster in the cafeteria. He took him over to the back to Faid, Nathaneal and Blue.

"Why is Gloughster here?" asked Faid standing up.

"The Emperor needs his Trance Channeler," said Gloughster.

"Stop that," said Lino and sat down. He pulled at Gloughster to sit but he wouldn't.

"Why is there a Trance Channeler here?" asked a mechanic at another table.

Suddenly someone came running into the cafeteria and yelled, "the Emperor is here!"

The cafeteria began to get noisy as people started in on why the Emperor would be here.

"You are my knight Faid, tell Gloughster he is crazy," said Lino. Faid looked up at Gloughster.

"Lino is the Emperor," is all Gloughster said. Someone sitting close to them heard him and started whispering to the people near him. Part of the table turned around and looked at Lino.

The battleship's communication line came on. "This is your Captain speaking. The 59th Emperor of the Pacific Territories is here on the Escalon. Please show him your respect. There will be an inspection in the hangar in one hour. Please dress appropriately."

The cafeteria became a jumble with activity. People started looking at Lino as they passed by and went to leave.

"Gloughster, come with me," Lino dragged Gloughster behind him. People started commenting and pointing at them as they moved down the hall into Lino's room. Lino closed the door as they arrived.

"Gloughster, what is going on?"

"Izen, my designation is Izen," sadi Gloughster.

"Fine Izen, why are you here?" asked Lino.

"The Emperor needs his Trance Channeler."

"Stop it Gloughster, this is crazy. When did this happen?"

"Two weeks ago your Majesty."

"Two weeks?" Lino was shocked.

Someone knocked at the door and called out. It sounded like Faid. Lino opened the door and Faid was wearing the uniform of the Elite Imperial Guard.

"Why did you change your clothes?"

"I was asked to by one of the ministers," sadi Faid.

A few people walking by saw Faid in his uniform and looked in the room. Lino could hear them.

"I think he really is the Emperor," said the people as they walked by.

"You mean the Emperor was here the whole time and we didn't know it?" They continued down the hall.

Shennen followed Faid into the room. He was carrying a ceremonial sword in his hand. He stepped up to Faid and fastened it around his waist. Faid just let him do it.

"You are the head of the Imperial Guard now Faid. What is your last name?"

"Callen," said Faid.

"Commander Callen, the Elite Guard is under your command."

"This is crazy," said Lino again. "What, is he a citizen too?"

"That is up to you, your Majesty," sadi Shennen.

"Okay, then he is a citizen."

"We will make sure the paperwork gets done," said Shennen.

"I know you always wanted that Faid," sadi Lino.

"It is time to go to the inspection," said Shennen who moved over to Lino and put officers bars on his shoulder and then put starts on his epaulets.

Faid and Lino walked to the hangar with Shennen and Gloughster following them. Shennen stopped Lino before he went into the hangar. He straightened Lino's cap and brushed off his shoulders, pushed Gloughster through the door and then went himself. Faid would go in front of Lino. He told Lino to wait until Faid reached where he should stand. Lino was announced. The Imperial anthem came over the communication line. Lino walked into the hangar, past the crowd and then came to stand beside Faid. There were a lot of whispers from the crowd. They had no idea the Emperor had been here the whole time. Lino just stood there and let the whispers come. Lino moved over to Shennen and whispered to him.

"Squadron and mechanic leads please step forward," said Shennen.

Fred, Blue and the rest of the people called came forward. Lino sent to Fred.

Did Sati fail his mental exam?

Yes, Sati failed his mental exam, sent Fred.

"Sati Ima step forward," said Lino.

Sati came through the crowd and stepped up next to Fred.

"Someone give me a set of wings," said Lino.

Someone came up to Lino and handed him a set of wings.

"Sati Ima are you crazy?" asked Lino.

The crowd laughed.

"Yes sir, I failed my mental exam four times in a row," said Sati.

Lino sent to Nathaneal. **Will you watch him carefully and make sure he stays safe?**

Yes, I will, sent Nathaneal.

"Sati Ima, you will take your mental exam everyday until you pass it so that you can fly to the satisfaction of your squadron lead. You have your wings back but you need to pass that test." Lino walked up to Sati and pinned the wings onto his uniform. Sati bowed and almost started to cry. Lino stepped back.

"I want to thank the squadron leads, the technical team and the mechanics for their hard work in making the Escalon a significant force in the Esset battle fleet. It is an honor to fly with you," said Lino.

Whispers started going off in the crowd again. Lino could hear them but just let them continue. Shennen stepped up and began speaking.

Silence! sent Faid to the entire hangar. The whispering stopped.

"That red haired guy is his knight. I thought he had an attitude. He is a crap pilot. I have seen him fly," said someone from the crowd.

"Hey!" Faid spoke up and walked past Shennen and into the crowd and pulled the guy out who said that and dragged him up in front of Lino.

"You, apologize to the Emperor," said Faid and put his hand on the guy's head and made him bow.

"I am sorry your majesty," said the pilot.

Lino didn't say anything, Faid pushed the guy back into the crowd. Shennen continued his speech. Gloughster walked past Shennen and put his hand up and began to speak when Shennen was done.

"The Emperor is satisfied with your progress. You are all blessed by the Prophets."

Shennen tapped Lino on the shoulder and he left with him out of the hangar followed by Faid and Gloughster. The crowd in the hangar started to break up and talk about the Emperor.

"He is young to be the Emperor."

"He is an Isshin pilot."

"He has been here the whole time and no one knew. That was pretty humble of him. I like that."

Sati failed his mental exam six more times. He was in his cabin and was angry with himself. He sparked up his aegis because he wanted to see. It was blue and orange. It was getting better but he was still not 100%. Nathaneal came into the room in his flight suit. He just came back to get something. He was going up.

"How did you do?"

"I failed again," Sati kicked his boot across the room.

"Can't you just memorize the questions?"

"They change the questions so I can't do that. Or they rephrase them differently. I forget the answers."

"How do you feel?"

"I want to fly and I can't go up. I should have just stayed out for the month."

"It is better to try. I am glad that Lino gave you the chance. Now that we know he is the Emperor I wonder if Fred will treat him differently."

"Is the Streak still out here?" asked Sati.

"Yes, I think he is waiting for you. They painted the yellow circle on your new Isshin. It looks good. I think they really souped it up. You are lucky. It is completely refurbished and it looks awesome. I think it is a newer model," said Nathaneal.

"Fred won't even let me go down there. They turned me out of the hangar when I tried to go down there yesterday."

"Fred is serious. I got to go. Lino is having some problems as well. I think the death of his father has affected him," said Nathaneal and left the cabin.

Nathaneal went to the hangar. The pilots from a few squadrons were circled around Fred. He was giving a briefing. The Escalon had left the battle fleet and was traveling farther into the Atlantic Ocean by itself.

"Blue, your squadron will fly backup for the Isshins."

"Why do we need backup?" asked Nathaneal.

"The Emperor is in your squadron," said Fred.

"I don't want any special treatment. I can hold my own," said Lino. He had been depressed ever since he had found out that his father was dead. That was two parents he never really got to mourn properly.

"This is not coming from me. This is coming from the Esset Commander," said Fred.

Sati came walking up to them. He was in his uniform.

"Sati, why are you here?" asked Fred.

"I can listen. I just can't fly," said Sati. They had let him in the hangar. They were not paying attention. Fred continued.

"Sam, your squadron will be aligning with Blue in a support role only." Sam nodded. Faid was in Sam's squadron. The whole squadron was new pilots. This was going to be one of the first runs that Sam's squadron would make. "The Atlantea Federation group will be coming from their base in one of these islands. We don't know exactly where. Be ready. They could sneak up on you. Pilots to your frames," said Fred.

Fred's squadron was launched second. Lino was worried. He came over the comm.

"I have a bad feeling about this."

"What is wrong Lino?" asked Fred over the comm.

"Something is not right. Where is Blue?" Lino fiddled with the comm and brought up Blue's squadron frequency so that he could join the conversation.

"Blue, do you feel something?" asked Lino.

Blue sent out his psi to the local vicinity and picked up a feeling. He couldn't pinpoint it but there were definitely emotions coming in that were out of the ordinary.

"There is something but I don't know what it is," said Blue his voice reverberating.

"Fred we need to be careful," said Lino.

"Keep the line open. I want us communicating," said Fred.

Fred's squadron with Blue's trailing did not encounter anything for some time. Then suddenly there were 50 frames on them.

"Engage!" yelled Fred and the two squadrons went after the bandits.

The battle was brutal. The 50 frames were hacking the Escalon's frames to shreds. Sam recalled Faid and he was sent back to the Escalon. The rest of Sam's squadron were picked off one by one. Faid was the only one left. Then Sam was taken out.

Lino was being chased by two frames. He transformed and flew off in aicraft mode. His pursuers followed suit. They had him locked on. One of them fired a missile, Lino came off high right and avoided it but the missile turned and chased him.

"Damn," said Lino. He pushed the machine synch button and the frame zoomed forward. The missile kept on him. Lino took a wide turn and went directly towards a group of enemy frames. He flew right by the formation, just barely keeping from hitting one of the planes to try and confuse the missile. It hit another frame and blew it up.

Raven's frame was fighting a red frame. He swung the sword module and cut off the frame's arm. It lost the sword. Raven fired the guns. The frame pilot ejected. Raven transformed and flew off.

The Atlantea Federation frames destroyed 80% of the Escalon's frames. Fred called a retreat. The Escalon frames ran. The Jannai picked off some on the way out. Blue's frame was hit. He was screaming. He had been hit in the face with metal from the cockpit and plastic from the helmet. He put his hand up over his eye. His face was bleeding.

They brought the frames in and Fred called all the pilots over. Blue had his hands up over his eye, holding his helmet and he was slightly bent over. Faid came to him and asked if he was ok.

"It burns!" screamed Blue. Fred waved Blue off he wanted him to get checked out. Faid went with him.

"We took a significant loss today. I don't want you to get defeated. Please register your IFF when you check in so that we can get an accurate count of the losses."

"Sir, the Escalon is by itself out here now. How are we going to defend ourselves against an onslaught like that again?" asked Raven.

"After that we will probably go rejoin the fleet. I don't know," said Fred. He was a little concerned about that actually.

Anis had gone to the Jannassee Islands. He returned with Shennen and the Elite Imperial Guard. Anis had been made the Viceroy and was going to take care of all the business. Lino would be staying with the Escalon. The Escalon rejoined the Esset battle group. They had wanted to find the base but had not been able to. It was too dangerous to leave the Escalon out there by itself after it had lost 80% of its pilots.

The Ready Room was virtually empty now that the squads had been decimated. There was some shuffling as they tried to get squads together with the remaining pilots. Fred didn't know if he wanted to split the squads into smaller groups or not. Out of the 30 pilots that had gone up there were only 7 left.

Sati finally passed his mental exam. It was a conditional pass if he had missed one more question he would have failed. He was in the Ready Room sitting next to Faid.

"What squadron are you in?"

"I think there is only Fred or Blue now," said Faid.

Sati sparked up his aegis. He wanted to see what colour it was. It was still orange.

"Put that out," said Nathaneal coming into the Ready Room and moving into that aisle where Sati and Faid were. "Do you want him to see you? Come on Sati think."

Sati put his head down like he had been scolded and sat up straight in the chair. Nathaneal sat down next to him and grabbed his hand.

"I get to fly again," said Sati.

"You passed?" asked Nathaneal turning towards him.

"Yes, I passed."

"Congratulations Sati."

"Sorry I missed the slaughter. That must have been brutal."

"It was. They shot down all the new pilots except for me. Sam saved my arse by calling me back in," said Faid.

"Why did we go out there anyway?" asked Sati.

Lino turned around from the seats in front of them, leaned in and explained. "The ministers wanted us to go on some happy hunting trip to find some base. We got slaughtered because it was stupid. I told them that we should have listened to Commander Ima but they overrode me."

"I thought you were the Emperor?" asked Sati.

"I am the Emperor but it is nothing more than a symbolic title. My cousin Anis went with the ministers. He is the Viceroy. They are running everything. I didn't want to get trapped in the Jannassee Islands. I wanted to remain here."

"So you bailed on your responsibility?" asked Sati.

"Sati stop. That is inappropriate," said Nathaneal.

Lino didn't say anything for a moment. "No, he is right. I did bail on my responsibility. My Trance Channeler told me this would eat me alive. My cousin is more suited for that kind of stuff anyway. It has to be someone in the family. And it is safer if I am out here. I can't get assassinated. Just shot down, I guess." Raven turned around.

"You guess?" said Raven. "You almost got your arse blown off from that missile if I understand correctly."

"So, I got out of it."

"You need to be more careful. You are the Emperor. You're lucky they haven't grounded you actually. I would. You are a head of state. You can't be flying around up here with us like that."

Fred had overheard Raven.

"Actually, Raven is right. We should probably ground you," said Fred.

"Don't do that," said Lino. Fred went to the head of the room and stood behind the podium and put his hands down on it and leaned in.

"I can't afford to do that though," said Fred then continued. "Faid, you are on full status now, you are no longer a trainee."

"Yes sir," said Faid.

"Sati, nice to see you again. It has been a while," said Fred.

Lino started clapping and stood up, turned around and reached in to shake Sati's hand. "Nice job, you made me have to wait a while for it."

"Couldn't be helped, Sati had a bit of trouble taking the test." He put his hand behind his head and blushed.

"Okay, enough games. On to business." Fred went to the wall control and brought up a satellite aerial shot of a vessel with a plume of smoke coming out of it. "This is the Ishibashi science vessel. It has been incapacitated. It took a hit. The ship is listing. They are in hostile territory and have reported armed fighter jets have been patrolling the area. We are to fly cover for them."

"How many frames are we talking about?" asked Nathaneal.

Fred went back to the wall control and pulled up an image. He touched the screen and enlarged it.

"These shots are from a surveillance frame in the area," said Fred. There were about eight frames in the still shot. Then Fred changed the image and a white frame could be seen.

"Is that the Streak?" asked Sati.

"It can't be the same plane. You blew up the Streak," said Nathaneal.

"You mean there is more than one?" asked Lino.

"No, he came back after me. That could be him," said Sati.

"It is just probably another frame with the same markings," said Nathaneal.

"Zoom in," said Sati and stood up.

Fred put his fingers on the screen and moved the image down and zoomed in on the white frame. Sati put his hands on the back of Lino's chair and leaned forward and looked at the image for a while and squinted. Then something clicked.

"That is the Streak. It has the same tail markings and that red line on the side," said Sati.

"You are really obsessed with that plane," said Raven.

"I need to know who shot me down," said Sati and sat back down.

"That vessel is in hostile waters you do not want to get shot down out there," said Fred.

"When do we go?" asked Blue, he had a bandage over his right eye.

"I haven't decided if you are all going yet. I need Nathaneal, Jane and now Sati. Lino you are staying here with Faid. I don't want you two out there. And yes Lino, this is because of who you are."

"Come on," said Lino hitting the side of the chair next to him.

"No Lino, that would be asking for the Pacific Territories to lose the war if they got you."

"Anis is technically the Emperor, I am just a figured head."

"Do you think that matters," said Fred. "I think I need to ground you until we can get this straightened out."

Lino sat back in the chair. He knew that was going to happen. There was too much at stake for him to be flying around at all.

"Okay, go get setup. I will brief you again when we get in the hangar. There is some additional information you will need," said Fred.

"Too bad Emperor. It was nice flying with you while it lasted," said Faid slapping Lino in the arm.

Lino pushed him and then teleported to the Command Center. Gailen turned around and saw him.

"Your Majesty," Gailen bowed. The Captain stood up and saluted.

"I just got grounded," said Lino.

"We do not want the Emperor out in hostile territory where you can get shot down."

"This is all hostile territory," said Lino.

"This is a different situation," said the Captain. Lino turned around to him. The Captain came up to the strategy table that Gailen and some other officers were hovered around.

"The Ishibashi is here," the Captain pointed at the holographic map.

"What are all those other vessels?" asked Lino pointing at the blocks on the display.

"Those are the enemies," the Captain looked over at him.

"They are as good as dead," said Lino.

"Yes, they are."

"Then why are you sending out a squadron if you are just going to leave them out there?"

"Because we are going to sacrifice them," said the Captain.

"Why, shouldn't we save them?" asked Lino.

"The Ishibashi is a strategic science vessel. It cannot be captured there is proprietary information on board and Jaiz the Trance Channeler. She is very valuable."

"Why, what is her significance?" asked Lino.

"She was the last Converger," said the Captain.

"100 years ago?" asked Lino. He looked up at Gailen who nodded. Lino continued. "Can't we rescue her?"

"It is too dangerous to send a vessel in there," said the Captain.

The holographic map updated and the blocks surrounding the vessel Ishibashi moved in closer. There was a display in the table of the Ishibashi. It was still spewing smoke. Lino saw the frames launched out of the catapults from the forward windows of the Command Center tower.

Fred's frame had been loaded with a bomb.

"Do you want to stay and watch?" asked the Captain.

"You are sending my subjects to their graves. It is the least I can do," said Lino.

Gailen pushed some buttons and replaced the holgographic map with the satellite view of the Ishibashi.

Sati liked his new frame. It was more high tech than his previous Isshin. He needed to take some time and really get to know the machine better.

"Approaching the target," said Fred.

"Are we really going to blow them up?" asked Nathaneal.

An Atlantea Federation frame blew by the formation and did not engage.

"Do not engage," said Fred, he meant that for Sati.

Is it a single?" asked Sati wanting confirmation. Nathaneal check his instruments.

"No, there is another reading," said Nathaneal.

Sati picked up a sending.

Yellow circle...

The proximity alarm went off in Sati's cockpit. Then another alarm. The bandit had missile lock.

"Permission to engage," said Sati.

The frame fired its guns on Sati and then came up behind him close and leveled off. It was the Streak. It joined formation right off Sati's wing.

"He wants you to engage. He is screwing with you," said Nathaneal.

The Streak pulled back and had Sati perfectly in line for the kill.

Gailen changed the feed on the satellite display and they could see the formation coming towards the Ishibashi.

"That is one too many planes," said Lino. "Can you enlarge the feed?"

Gailen motioned one of the radar officers who came over to the strategy table and started to type in some commands and brought the image in closer.

"That is the Streak," said Lino. "He is on Sati again. What is with those two?"

"Approaching target," said Fred. "Payload armed."

The Streak transformed and loaded its sword module still keeping up with the formation and then wildly swung at Sati's frame and broke off part of the wing.

"Shit," Sati gripped the stirrup controls and the frame started shaking in the sky. He was trying to get a handle on it. Nathaneal slowed down and left formation. He was going to go to Sati's aid if he needed it. Fred did not stop him. He had a mission to accomplish. Fred pulled forward and moved over the target. The targeting computer confirmed the lock and he dropped the bomb. The Streak transformed again and stayed just on Sati. He still had missile lock.

"He is going to engage when the Ishibashi blows," said Nathaneal. "Be ready for it."

Sati turned off the limiter and moved a little forward. The Streak was on him tight.

The Ishibashi blew up. The Streak fired. Sati banked. The Streak went after him fully aggressive. Sati pulled back on the stirrup controls and arched the frame stopping his trajectory. The Streak blew right by him. Sati fired and hit the Streak who transformed.

"Do not engage here," said Fred. "Get out of hostile waters. I cannot send someone to rescue you out here."

"Understood," came Sati and banked and came back in. The Streak followed him. Nathaneal followed Sati and the Streak.

"Permission to engage," came Nathaneal.

"You have not been fired upon," came Fred.

The Streak locked on. He had the perfect shot. Then he just disengaged.

"Return to base," came over the comm line.

"Mission accomplished your Majesty," said Gailen.

"You just killed my subjects. What type of mission was that?"

"It was necessary," said the Captain.

An officer came up to the Captain with a phone, "Commander Ima, sir." The captain took the phone and walked off.

"You have to let me fly again," said Lino to Gailen. "I can't be sitting up here doing nothing."

"We just didn't want you over that area. The Ishibashi didn't just roam into hostile waters. They knew that this might be the outcome. The Commander was well aware of that."

"I have had enough politics for the day," said Lino and walked out of the Command Center and back to his cabin. Gloughster and Saya were in his room.

Lino walked up the Gloughster and hugged him. He wanted to be close to him. It had been a long time since they had been together. Lino also noticed that Gloughster had been jacked.

"You look good your Majesty," said Saya.

"It has been a while Saya. How do you like being on a battleship?" asked Lino.

"It is strange your majesty but Gloughster is making it so I am not scared."

Lino just realized her hair was white now.

"What happened to your hair Saya?"

"I am degenerating," she said.

"Why, what happened?"

"I gave my life force to Gloughster so that he could evolve."

"You did what?" asked Lino.

"For a Trance Channeler to serve the Emperor the life of their Adept is forfeit. That life force is taken for the second stage of evolution," said Gloughster with no emotion.

"Saya, did you agree to this?" asked Lino.

"It was not a question of agreeing. When you became the Emperor, Gloughster was forced as your Trance Channeler to make the transition. There was no choice to be made. My entire life has been in the service of Gloughster as his Adept. I knew that this could happen."

"Gloughster, you did not tell me this."

"We did not think we had to worry about it. You were just the Viceroy. But now you are the Emperor."

"Saya, I need to talk to Gloughster. Can you leave us alone for a while."

Saya smiled and left the cabin.

"Did you have the Emperor assassinated?" asked Lino.

"Why do you ask that," Gloughster wanted to know.

Lino got angry. He could feel Gloughster's mind. He had tapped him again the moment he saw him. There was something in his mind now. He felt like Justine. "Gloughster, I can feel you what did you do?"

"We took out the faction that was fanning the flames of war."

Lino sparked up his aegis and advanced on Gloughster.

"You killed my father?" Lino screamed at the top of his lungs. He threw lightening at Gloughster who blocked it with his hand. Lino just looked at him. How had he done that.

"The Trance Channeler needs to be just as powerful as the Emperor."

"What did you do Gloughster?"

"Chris jacked up my psi on your construct but you are still more powerful than me."

Chapter 8

"Gloughster why did you kill my father?" asked Lino.

"I told you we wanted to stop the war."

"And did that happen Gloughster, you tell me. Did that happen? Why are we out here in the Atlantic Ocean then? Who told you to do that, Chris? Did Jai lose control and Escani is running the show?"

Gloughster looked away. What Lino had guessed was probably true, he knew how Gloughster acted when he didn't want to have to lie.

"Your father handed the Astair Islands to the Atlantea Federation. It took away our strategic advantage in the south. That needed to be remedied."

"And did killing him remedy that?" Lino was beside himself. He had a difficult relationship with his father but he didn't want him dead.

"Lino, your father was compromised, he needed to be taken out to ensure that the Pacific Territories did not come under the control of the Atlantea Federation. He knew the risks as the Emperor."

"So you sacrificed him. That is the second sacrifice I have heard of on this day. I don't like politics."

"As the Emperor you need to be able to deal with high politics like this," said Gloughster.

"So are you going to sacrifice me as well?"

"If we have to then that is a possibility, but right now you need to handle the Convergence when it comes. You are too valuable, more valuable as the Converger than as the Emperor."

"Fine Gloughster, get out!" Lino screamed and pointed towards the door.

Gloughster did not move. Lino walked over to the door and opened it. "Get out!" he pointed. People in the hall heard him and stopped looking into the room.

"Trance Channeler, I order you to get out of this room!"

"Yes, your Majesty," said Gloughster and started walking towards the door. He seemed to float now. Lino had no idea what taking Saya's life force had done to him or how powerful he was now. Saya was outside in the hall.

"Do not come back here until you learn your place!" screamed Lino.

"The emperor is mad," said someone in the hall.

"Saya, get in here," Lino ordered her. Saya came walking in the door. Lino slammed the door behind Gloughster. He stayed out in the hall.

"Who are you loyal to Saya? Will you follow the request of your Emperor or will you side with your Trance Channeler?" asked Lino and folded his arms across his chest and waited.

Saya actually hesitated. "I am loyal to the Emperor, your Majesty."

"What has gotten into Gloughster? How could he take out my father?"

Saya started to cry.

"Justine is gone too your Majesty."

Lino hesitated he did not understand why Saya was crying.

"Why are you crying Saya?" Lino leaned in to her and hugged her. She buried her face in his chest and put her hands up to him.

"I felt her die your Majesty because I was connected to her as well. Just like I am connected to Gloughster," she said through her tears.

"They took out the Trance Channeler too?"

"The Emperor goes the Trance Channeler goes that is the tradition. Gloughster is tied to you, your Majesty. He will become ruthless and fight for you. You will become his entire life. He is loyal to you by his bond. He will die for you if need be," said Saya.

"Why is this happening?" asked Lino. He didn't understand. "Is this why Shennen came here with the Imperial Guard to bring Gloughster here?"

"The Trance Thanneler directs things by his will. He is dealing with politics as we speak your Majesty and directing the flow of the Pacific Territories. It is the same as in the Atlantea Federation. Gloughster is very powerful now. The ministers may be in charge but Gloughster is directing the outcome via the timestream," said Saya. "And there is something else..."

"What is it Saya?" Lino did not like the way that sounded.

"You must establish the bond with him your Majesty and then you must mate with me and I must bear your child. You must have a son. He can guarantee that now."

"Saya what are you saying?" Lino backed away from her.

"It is the rule your Majesty. That is why all Adepts are female."

"I will not do that Saya."

"You must," she said and Gloughster appeared in the room.

"I told you to get out," said Lino angrily.

"No, now you must listen to me," said Glougshter. "The

Emperor must have an heir. There is no getting around this. It is the law. She will bear your child."

"No, Gailen will tell you that is crazy Gloughster," said Lino.

"Gailen already knows that this is necessary."

"I will not do that," Lino crossed his arms. Gloughster held his hand out and took control of Lino who moved towards Saya and pushed her down on the bunk bed. Lino started to remove her clothes. "I will not do this Gloughster."

"Yes, you will," said Gloughster and exerted more control over him. Saya pulled up her dress and leaned down on the bed.

Gloughster moved Lino like a puppet and went through the motions and Lino slept with Saya, Gloughster standing over them the whole time directing the encounter. Lino tried to resist him but he could not. Gloughster when it was done came over to Saya and put his hand on her forehead and manipulated her biologically. He had Lino pull up his pants and then released him. Lino walked up to him and slapped him hard in the face.

"How dare you!" Lino screamed at him zipping up his pants and fastening his belt. Saya was crying. Lino had hurt her.

"You must mate with him now," said Saya standing up and wiping the tears off her face.

"I will not," yelled Lino.

"Lino you must. He has evolved. You don't know how powerful he is now."

Gloughster put his hand out again and took control of Lino who tried to spark up his aegis but could not resist him. He unbuckled his belt and pulled off his pants and sat down on the bed.

"Don't do it like that Gloughster. Let him make the decision," said Saya. "You must do this Lino."

"How can this be the tradition?" asked Lino.

Gloughster stepped out of the Trance Channeler jumpsuit and cape and put it down on the top bunk.

"You are a monster," said Lino.

"He is a Trance Channeler Lino. This is what they do. They direct the world. It is a means to an end," said Saya.

"We are all pawns in their game," said Lino.

Gloughster released him and asked Saya to leave the room. Gloughster came to sit in his underwear next to Lino. Saya shut the door behind her.

"I thought you couldn't feel because of the pain from the psi conditioning?" asked Lino.

"That is behind me. I have evolved," said Gloughster. He put his hand on Lino's shoulder. Lino brushed him off.

"Why did you have me do that to Saya?"

"Because you would never have slept with her if I had not done that. We will do this the way it has to be done."

Gloughster leaned in to Lino and pushed him back on the bed. Lino layed on his back and just looked up at him. He had missed Gloughster but he did not like this new power he had.

"You have changed Gloughster. You need to be more gentle, like you were before."

"I am a Trance Channeler Lino. We are not gentle." Gloughster put his hand out and his nails grew and he ripped up Lino's shirt and scratched him. Lino's eyes got wide. He was going to get hurt. Gloughster sparked up his aegis and grabbed Lino by the throat and turned him over and thrust his head back down on the bed. Gloughster put his hand on Lino's back and made him release his wings. Gloughster ripped up his back.

"I am going to rape you like Isk did," said Gloughster and reached in and pulled feathers out of Lino's wings. Lino cried out. Gloughster put his hand on the back of Lino's head and knocked him out with a psi pulse so that he couldn't feel anything. Then he raped him. He was brutal and ripped up his back with his nails and left it a bloody mess. Gloughster put his Trance Channeler jumpsuit back on and the cape then opened the door. Saya was standing outside the door with a towel.

"He needs some looking after," said Gloughster.

"Were you cruel to him like Isk was?" she asked.

"I knocked him out. That was the best I could do for him. I still care about him Saya no matter what I am now required to do. He is my Lord and I will do my best to protect him but we needed to get that out of the way."

"I understand but now this piece is done. Do not treat him like that again," she said scolding him.

"I will do my best Saya. Take care of him now so that he can be presentable. I will get Raven to heal him." Gloughster walked away and closed the door behind him. Lino was unconscious as Saya tended to his back. His wings were still out.

"Lino, Lino..." Saya called out to him. He started to wake up. His body hurt. He retracted his wings.

"What happened?" Lino asked and sat up, he put his hand up to his head then put his hand on his back. It hurt. He looked at his hand and it was bloodied.

"Gloughster slept with you. He knocked you out so that it didn't hurt you."

"Why did he do that, sleep with me?"

"To re-establish the bond now that he has evolved." Saya put the towel on his back and patted it so that it soaked up the blood. Lino stood up and unbuttoned his shirt that was ripped now and took it off. Raven knocked on the door and called to Lino. Saya opened the door. Lino sat down on the bed and Raven sat behind him.

"What happened to you?" Raven could see his back all ripped up.

"My Trance Channeler happened to me," said Lino facing the desk. Raven put his hands on Lino's back and Lino flinched. Raven could see the very beginning of the encounter then it went blank because Lino had been out cold.

"Did he put you out and do this to you?" asked Raven.

"He didn't want Lino to feel it," said Saya.

"He did the same thing to you that Isk did," said Raven.

"Pretty much," said Lino as Raven healed his back. The flesh knitted back together. He still had some residual scarring from the last time this happened to him.

"I don't understand Trance Channelers," said Raven.

"I think I am beginning to and I don't like them much any more," said Lino.

Raven removed his hands. He had finished healing him and stood up. "Fred has been looking for you. I think he wants to talk about your flight status."

"Do you know where he is?"

"I think he is in the hangar. The rest of your squad has been down there with the maintenance crew. They are running maintenance checks," said Raven.

"Okay, thanks," said Lino. Raven turned to leave. Saya started to follow him.

"Are you okay Saya? I am so sorry this happened. I can hardly look at you. I can't believe I did that," said Lino.

"Lino, I know you never would have done that if he had not been controlling you," she said.

"You let me know if you need anything."

"No Lino, Gloughster will take care of it. It is not your concern anymore."

"How can you say that?"

"This is just how it will be handled your Majesty. They will not bother you with this again. When the time comes they will take me away from here and you will not see me again. This happened to your father as well when he became Emperor."

Saya turned to leave and walked out of the room. Lino changed his clothes. He put on a t-shirt and went to the hangar. Fred was with some maintenance technicians near his frame. Lino walked up to him. Fred was holding up a maintenance tablet. The technician called to the mechanic to make a change. Lino could see Sati over by his frame. He was up on the ramp with the technician and pointing into the cockpit. There must have been someone inside. Fred turned around when he saw Lino.

"Where is your uniform?" asked Fred.

"I think I need a new shirt. I kind of had an accident."

"Ok, we can get that for you."

"I wanted to check on my flight status," said Lino.

"The Captain is waiting input from your Trance Channeler. You cannot fly until he has cleared you."

"My Trance Channeler?"

"Yes, that is what he said. You can join us in the maintenance checks if you want, but it is not mandatory. You will need to do it by the end of the week though."

"Alright then, I will do it later," said Lino and patted Fred on the shoulder and went to the Command Center.

Gloughster was not in the Command Center. Lino had released his tap on him when Gloughster had knocked him out. Lino psi located him. He was in the living quarters but in another cabin. Lino went to the room and teleported in. Gloughster was sitting on the bed crying and there was a hyper inject syringe with a vial of juice in it next to him on the bed. Gloughster looked up at Lino with tears in his eyes and then waved him off and put his head in his hands. Lino felt bad. He moved over to Gloughster and sat down next to him.

"What is wrong?" asked Lino.

Gloughster didn't say anything for a while. He picked up the juice syringe and shot himself up in the palm of his hand. "I was terrible to you and to Saya. I did unspeakable things and I was cruel about it."

"Saya said it had to be done. You said that," said Lino. He wiped the tears off Gloughster's cheeks.

"I hurt you."

Lino put his hand on Gloughster's knee. "Yes, you did." Lino stood up. He was still angry.

"The evolution makes me crazy. It makes me do things. The timestream is relentless. I cannot turn it off. It is always present and urgent. I have to deal with it all the time."

"I knew that was not like you. You are a gentle soul," said Lino.

Gloughster stood up and moved over to Lino and hugged him. He put his head down on Lino's shoulder. "If I get out of hand you have to tell me. You have to stop me from hurting you like that again. I am more powerful now with the evolution. The amount of power that I have to deal with now is excrutiating. How can you handle this level of power? It feels like it is swallowing me."

"I hardly notice it."

"Then you are much stronger than I am," said Gloughster.

"How did you stop the lightening from before?" asked Lino.

"I am a foil to you now. There are certain things that I can do that will keep both our codess in check. You probably could have resisted me if you had been given a chance."

"How could you control me like that? Especially if my level is higher than yours."

"We are connected."

"Then let me fly."

"That is not wise."

"I order you," said Lino.

"Yes, your Majesty."

"You must communicate this to the Captain."

"If we go up in hostile waters I will ground you again. We cannot have you captured."

"Gloughster, why did you need to mate with me like that? We could have done it pleasantly, I would have allowed it."

"It was not going to be pleasant your Majesty. I was completely controlled by the codess you could not have stopped me. I am sorry, I knew I was going to hurt you. That is why I didn't want you to be awake for it."

"I think that made it worse actually," said Lino. "Don't do that again."

"Yes, your Majesty."

Lino turned to leave.

"I love you," said Gloughster.

Lino walked out without saying a word.

Lino just came from being up in the Isshin for some reconnaissance. He had gone up with Sati. They were in the locker room together putting on their uniforms. Lino had his back to Sati.

"Where did you get all those scars on your back from?" asked Sati pulling on his shirt and buttoning it.

"I had a run in with a Jannai," said Lino. He took his shoes out of the locker and put them on the floor.

"That looks pretty bad. When did that happen?"

"At the Psi Faction a few months ago. How are you doing?" Lino did not want to talk about that anymore.

Sati sat down and tied his shoes as Lino sat down next to him.

"I am not hallucinating really anymore but I am still a little scared."

"That has to be hard for you," said Lino.

"It is just that it is unpredictable," said Sati standing up and closing his locker.

"Want to come with me to the cafeteria? I need to eat something. I am starving," said Lino.

"Sure." They started walking to the cafeteria.

"Are you really getting to go on leave soon?" asked Lino.

"Yes, I have always wanted to go to Shion. We should be coming up on it in a few days. Nathaneal thought that going ashore would be good therapy for me," said Sati.

"This is not really friendly territory. Shion is not an enemy state. I believe it is neutral," said Lino.

"You should come with us."

"I don't think the Emperor gets to just go wandering around in another country. It could have political implications. But I can always ask I guess."

Faid was in the cafeteria with Blue who still had a bandage over his eye. Lino ordered Selat and sat down next to Faid who had a tablet next to him.

"What are all those?" asked Lino.

Sati picked up the tablet and looked at one of the books on Faid's list. The title of the book read 'Quadrion Frame Technical Schematic.'

"I have homework. Fred wanted me to get familiar with the manuals. He said I have to take a test on this to get some certification," said Faid.

"Yeah, I remember that," said Sati. "How long till you have to take the test?"

"I have a week I think," said Faid.

"You have to read all that. I didn't have to do that," said Lino.

"He is a newbie. You probably had to take it back at the Psi Faction," said Sati.

"I don't think so. I didn't have to take any test," said Blue.

The intercom came on, "Ameliano Dejarre to the Command Center."

Lino got up from the table. He hadn't been able to eat. He put the cover on the dish and took it with him.

"You are going to the Command Center with foor?" asked Faid.

"No, I am going to put it in the room. I am starving." Lino left and went back to his room first before going to the Command Center.

When he got to the Command Center Gloughster was there. Lino walked up to Gailen and looked at the holographic map. It read 'Shion' on the side and there was an image of what looked like a palace in one of the corners.

"Your Majesty," said the Captain.

"What do you need?" asked Lino. Gailen spoke up.

"We would like you to go to the royal palace in Shion. This is a diplomatic visit. Shion is requesting entry into the Pacific Territories."

"I thought Shion was neutral?" asked Lino.

"It was until they were attacked by the Atlantea Federation last month," said the Captain. "They were able to hold off the attack and keep from being occupied but they are requesting to officially be brought into the fold."

"Shion is a little too close to the Atlantea Federation for my tastes. Are you sure you want me to go there?" asked Lino.

"The Atlantea Federation will not attack Shion again. They have what they came for," said Gloughster.

"What did they attack for then?" asked Lino.

"They went after a Trance Channeler. It was in the timestream."

"Shion is a very religious country. They honor the prophets. They are mostly a pacifist nation. They probably just handed over the Trance Channeler instead of fighting," said Gailen.

"We would like Faid to go with you," said the Captain.

"As my knight?" asked Lino.

"Not exactly. We want him to go because he is a Packrat. There are a lot of Packrats in Shion," said Gloughster.

"I did not know that there were Packrats in other places, just in the Echelons and the Zone," said Lino.

"Faid is actually the leader for the entire Packrat clan around the world. That is why they were such a powerful terrorist organization," said Gailen. "The Packrats have been helping the Pacific Territories around the globe."

"Wow, I should treat him with some more respect," said Lino.

"Faid Callen to the Command Center," came over the intercom. Faid looked over at Blue.

"You have got to be kidding me. What do they want me for?" Faid said. "I don't even know where the Command Center is." Faid sent to Lino and psi located him. He left the tablet in the cafeteria with Blue and materialized in the Command Center.

"We need a favor from you as a Packrat," said the Captain.

"Okay," said Faid, he did not know where this was going.

"Who is the head of the Packrats in Shion?" asked Gailen.

"That I will not tell you," said Faid. He did know.

"We need you to accompany his Majesty to the Shion palace to meet with the head of that country. As I understand the Packrats are very close to the political structure in Shion," said Gailen.

"That is true," said Faid. "They will know I am coming."

"Shion has requested to join the Pacific Territories. We would like a representative of the Packrats there at the meeting."

"That can be arranged," said Faid. "When do we reach Shion?"

"Tomorrow," said the Captain.

"Do you have a handheld I can contact them?" asked Faid.

"No, but I have a sat phone," said Gailen.

Gailen handed the phone to Faid who dialed a number that could not be traced and bounced off multiple satellites and masked threw a few other numbers. It rang and Faid started talking in code. He said 'Shion' was the only thing that Lino understood. Acolyte answered back. Faid put his hand over the phone and asked Gailen when they would be going.

"We will be in close enough to shuttle you over tomorrow morning," said the Captain.

Faid started speaking into the phone again. Acolyte was communicating with Shion as they were speaking. He had a hacker in their system almost immediately. Faid waited for a while, said something more then hung up.

"It is arranged. There will be a Packrat representative there to meet us. I will not be going as a member of the military, I will be going as a Packrat," said Faid and handed the phone back to Gailen.

SATI IMA IN THE COCKPIT OF THE QUADRION ISSHIN IN AN AERIAL DOG FIGHT WITH THE STREAK, AN ATLANTEA FEDERATION FRAME.

Chapter 9

Sati and Nathaneal went into Shion in the afternoon. The Escalon docked and they disembarked relatively early on once they landed. Sati insisted on wearing his uniform. Nathaneal just wore street clothes. They went to a temple near the dock as their first stop. Shion was a very religious country and there were temples and shrines located all over the landscape. Sati had been to a Prophet temple multiple times before and for the mate pair ceremony. He wanted to check out the monks.

When they arrived there was a large bell at the entrance to the temple grounds. Sati wanted to ring the bell but instead they went over to the prayer wheel. Sati pushed it around in a circle and recited a prayer as he went. Then they went to the wishing stone and wrote a wish on a small piece of paper and put it in the stone. Sati wanted to get the Streak. That was his wish. Nathaneal wished to be happy for the rest of his life and spend it with Sati. They went inside and watched part of the prayer meditation with the monks chanting and then went into town.

"Come on, hurry up Nathaneal," said Sati as he waved him over to one of the bike drawn rickshaws. Nathaneal had stopped and was talking to a shop clerk. He had seen something in the window he wanted. He went inside of her shop and bought the item then went back to Sati.

"Give me your hand," said Nathaneal. Sati stuck out his hand and Nathaneal put a bracelet on his wrist that looked like it was made of small gold coins with a red rope braided around them.

"What is it?" asked Sati.

"It is a Hailan amulet. It will keep you safe," said Nathaneal.

"Thanks Nathaneal, the Streak won't be able to get me now."

Nathaneal sat down next to Sati in the rickshaw and the driver started the motorcycle and they took off down the street.

A car met Faid and Lino at the dock. A minister stepped out and introduced himself then asked them to get inside the car. The car drove them to the palace. The minister seemed very interested in Faid in his Packrat attire.

"Are the Packrats part of the military?" asked the minister in the car on the ride over.

"Faid is my knight. He is accompanying me," said Lino.

"Oh, I understand. This is a pacifist nation. Shion does not have a military. The Packrats are the only fighting force that exists here."

"How does your country protect itself then?" asked Lino.

"The Packrats provide the security. They have frames and weapons. We leave the fighting up to them."

"Who is the government minister that we will be meeting?" asked Lino.

"You will be meeting the Crown Prince. I will need to translate for you. He does not speak the international language," said the minister.

The car came to stop in front of a lavish building at the bottom of a long staircase. The driver opened the door for them. Lino got out. It was warm in Shion. Lino was wearing his dress military uniform. Based on this meeting, Shion would be let into the Pacific Territories if Lino found their answers satisfactory. They walked up the large staircase and into the palace entry hall. There was a group of Packrats with a couple of ministers in the hall. Faid walked in behind Lino. The ministers bowed to Lino. The lead Packrat got down on one knee and put a fist at his chest. Faid walked over to the Packrats and started to speak in code. The lead Packrat answered him back and then put out his hand. Faid took his arm and held it in the Packrat salute then took a step back and the Packrat bowed to Faid. Lino continued down the hall with the ministers with Faid and the lead Packrat following behind.

They went into a room with a lavish embroidered carpet with a mandala on it. There was a round table in the middle of the room. Lino and Faid sat down with the ministers. The door opened and a boy came in accompanied by a woman in a lavish costume. The boy sat down and the woman stood behind him.

"This is his Majesty Clovis Regne, the Crown Prince of Shion."

"He is only a child," said Faid.

Lino looked over at Faid appalled.

"Forgive my knight your Majesty. He did not mean to be rude," said Lino looking over at Faid.

"He does not understand you," said the minister next to Lino. "But thank you for the words."

"Who is this?" asked the child in his native language. It sounded like singing to Lino.

The minister explained Lino and Faid in the native language of Shion. The child could see that Faid was a Packrat and he got up and walked over to Faid, touched his hands and started talking.

"He wants to see the colour of your aegis," said the minister.

Faid sparked up his aegis. It was purple due to the kedek infusion. The child looked at Faid's hands as Faid turned his hands over for the child to see. The other Packrat began speaking to the child. He told him that Faid was the head of the Packrats around the world. The child's smile grew and he seemed to be really happy. The child began to speak quickly. The minister tried to translate and keep up. The child turned to Lino and hesitated for a moment then asked a question.

"His Majesty would like to ask for permission to join the Pacific Territories," translated the minister, "but he is scared that you will not accept him."

"Why is he concerned we will not accept Shion?" asked Lino.

"Because they gave the Trance Channeler to the Atlantea Federation. It was Jaiz, the last converger's servant," said the minister in a strong accent.

Lino picked up a sending from Gloughster.

**Shion should not be allowed to join the Pacific Territories unless they can guarantee their neutrality. Now that the Atlantea Federation have their Trance Channeler they are compromised."

"Explain to the Crown Prince that he must guarantee the neutrality of Shion for his country to be accepted into the Pacific Territories. The fact that he lost the Trance Channeler has made the acceptance unpredictable," said Lino.

The minister translated for the child who went back and sat down motioning to the woman beside the chair. He whispered to her and then she spoke.

"His Majesty understands that Shion has been compromised. He would like to ask the Packrats for their support in ensuring that they will keep their integrity."

The Packrat lead spoke up in code and looked at Faid who translated for Lino.

"Ain wants the Emperor to know that the Packrats have found where they are holding Jaiz' servant. They would like the Emperor's permission to go in and get him back."

"Why are they asking me?" asked Lino.

"Shion is a pacifist country. They cannot ask the Crown Prince for permission to attack," said Faid.

"Then I will authorize it. They must get Jaiz' servant back. Jaiz is gone. We have no other connection to the last Convergence without the servant. That is key," said Lino.

Faid translated in code. The Packrat acknowledged and put his hand at his chest in a fist. The Packrat lead and the Crown Prince stood up. Lino didn't understand but he guessed that the meeting was over. The child came over to Lino and took his hand and led him out of the room, down a long hall to what looked like a shrine. It was attached to the palace. The Packrat lead left them and Faid stayed with him. The minister followed the Crown Prince and Lino into the shrine. They walked up to a large kedek pool. The child spoke and the minister translated.

"He knows you are Jannai. He wants to see your wings," said the minister.

A Prophet came over dressed in black monks clothing. Lino was not about to show his wings to a child. The monk came up to Lino and raised his hand.

"Your Majesty," said the monk and moved in to put his hand on Lino's forehead. Lino took a step back. The monk hesitated and moved in again.

"It is customary to let the Prophets read your intentions. It will bode well for the process if the Prophets deem you genuine," said the minister.

Lino picked up a sending from Faid.. **You must pass their integrity test or Shion will become hostile to us very quickly. They are not on our side right now. They are waiting.**

"I will allow it," said Lino. The monk put his hand on Lino's forehead and his hair started to stand up as the monk channeled Lino's energy through the connection.

You have been mate paired to a Trance Channeler, sent the Prophet. He could see Gloughster in Lino's memories. Lino felt something odd about this connection. It was as if the Prophet was stealing his memories. He was searching for something. Suddenly the Prophet's eyes got wide and he released his hand and backed up, going down into kowtow position on the floor in front of Lino. The Crown Prince looked at him. The Prophet said something and then the Crown Prince got down on the floor as well as the minister.

"We will join the Pacific Territories if you will allow it. We did not know. We are sorry for having been rude your Majesty," said the minister from the floor.

Lino put his hand out to the Crown Prince to help him up. The Prince did not move.

"He will not move until you give him permission," said the minister.

Lino told the Crown Prince to get up and the minister translated. The Crown Prince stood up but kept his head bowed.

"Why is he acting like that?" asked Lino.

"Because you are the Converger. He is not worthy to be standing in front of the Converger. Asking you such questions before was rude. He is concerned that you will not allow Shion into the Pacific Territories now."

"If the Packrats can rescue Jaiz' servant we will allow Shion into the Pacific Territories. Even if they cannot we will allow Shion in. It is a strategic advantage," said Lino.

The minister stood up along with the Prophet. Lino received a sending from Faid.

The Packrats have Jaiz' servant.

How did they get him that fast? sent Lino.

They were waiting to go in. sent Faid.

So the servant was still in Shion? Does that mean the Atlantea Federation is still in Shion? Lino became worried.

"Excuse me your Majesty, you need to take us back to the harbor," said Lino.

Faid teleported to Lino and whispered to him, "there is hostile energy here."

Lino picked up a sending from Sati, **We were just recalled. Where are you?**

The minister dismissed himself from the Crown Prince and walked with Faid and Lino back to the car. The minister was not going back with them. He leaned into the driver's window and told the driver to take a direct route.

"He will take you quickly. We will notify your ship that you are coming," said the minister.

"Why did you not tell us that Shion still had Atlantea Federation factions here? Your entry into the Pacific Territories is not guaranteed," said Lino.

"We understand that. We will continue to petition for entry," said the minister.

"You should be very careful. Playing a game like that with the Emperor is not wise," said Faid.

There were Packrats outside the front of the palace with guns and knives. Faid could feel the communal sending. As the car drove back Faid filled in Lino with what he had learned.

"The Atlantea Federation never left Shion. They have been here the entire time since they attacked. They have control of the Crown Prince. I think the only reason you were allowed out of there is because you are the Converger. The country is going to fall the minute you leave here. The Packrats will do their best to keep the Atlantea Federation out of the area," said Faid.

"No matter how much I am okay with the Packrats the ministers will never allow a country controlled by Packrats to be part of the Pacific Territories. It is like recognizing a terror cell," said Lino.

"I give you my word," said Faid. "The Packrats will do nothing to compromise the Emperor's position."

The car arrived at the dock. Sati and Nathaneal were getting out of a rickshaw when Lino and Faid drove up. The driver let them out then sped away.

"They are really jumpy," remarked Lino.

"There were Packrats with guns in the city," said Sati as they walked back to the ship.

Lino heard gunfire off in the distance. The group walked back to the ship. There were armed guards at the ramp.

"Hurry up," the guards shuffled them forward.

"You need to go to the Command Center that is what the Captain said," remarked the guard.

Lino picked up a sending from Gloughster. He wanted to make sure Lino was safe.

Why did you send me in there? sent Lino.

Your safety was guaranteed, sent Gloughster.

That was dangerous.

The Packrats will guarantee that Shion remains neutral now that they have seen Faid. Faid has a lot of power. They know you are the Converger. They were just honored that you acknowledged them.

Gloughster cut off his sending. He was not in the Command Center when Lino got there.

The radar officer sounded the call, "we have multiple contacts."

Another officer took binoculars and looked out the front windows, "I don't see anything."

The Captain picked up the phone and called down to the hangar, "I want those frames up in the air." Lino had never heard the Captain be that informal. Something was going on.

"What is the concern?" asked Lino.

"We have multiple bogeys out past the geographic boundary."

Gloughster came into the Command Center and went over to the communications officer and told him to do something.

"You want me to do what?" said the communications officer really loud.

"I want you to do what I tell you," said Gloughster. "Tell them."

The communication officer looked over at the Captain before he did anything. Gloughster picked up the headset and put it in the officer's hand. The communications officer put the headset on his head and fixed the mic.

"This is ISS Escalon to Atlantea Federation flagship vessel, we have the Emperor of the Pacific Territories on board this vessel. Please acknowledge."

"What are you doing Gloughster?" asked Gailen. He was not happy.

It took some time and there was no response.

"They are changing course," said the radar officer.

Another radar officer confirmed multiple hits. "We have multiple bogeys at 9 miles."

Blue's squadron launched and could be seen out the forward Command Center windows.

Sati and Nathaneal went directly to the locker room and got suited up. They were in the hangar with Fred.

"I'm going," said Lino and started to walk out.

"No, you are staying here," said Gloughster. "You have to be part of the negotiations."

"Negotiations with whom?" asked Lino.

"With the Atlantea Federation and Isk," said Gloughster.

Lino cringed. "Isk is here?" Lino's back started to hurt him.

"We will get Shion to join the Pacific Territories or we will blow them off the face of the map and teach the Atlantea Federation a lesson."

"You are not going to sacrifice all those people?"

"Yes, I am," said Gloughster. "They were warned and they did not listen. Put Raven directly over the palace."

"What are you doing Gloughster?" asked Lino.

"Raven's frame has been loaded with a warhead. I will settle this if I have to in the most direct way possible. The Atlantea Federation cannot win here."

Raven had not launched yet. They were holding him back until they determined that he was needed. Blue's squadron had gone out and ran point. There were multiple bogeys at the staging area but they did not engage. The Captain left them out there for a while deciding what was the next step. An Atlantea Federation helicopter landed on the deck of the Escalon. Isk came out and was escorted to the officer's meeting room by armed guard. Gailen, Gloughster and Lino were already in the room. Faid came in the room dressed in Packrat attire.

"There is no representative of Shion here," whispered Lino. Isk had just come in the room.

"Faid is representing Shion and we will have some guests via satellite," said Gailen.

Faid had a handheld and the line was open. He sat down at the table. The heads up display came on and the minister and the lady who had been with the Crown Prince came on. Then a Packrat came on the other side of the screen. It was Ain who had been in the meeting earlier.

Isk sat down and looked over at Lino smiling wickedly. Lino felt uncomfortable. His back was hurting. He knew it was psychological but it did not stop him from feeling it. Gloughster began to speak.

"We have representation here from all the key players."

"The Atlantea Federation does not have a stake in Shion," said Isk.

Gloughster paused and turned very slowly to Isk and then elucidated each word. "The Atlantea Federation has occupied a neutral nation. You are in violation of the Armistice Agreement."

Isk put his hand on the table. "The Atlantea Federation has not occupied Shion."

"There is undue influence," said the minister on the video screen.

The Packrat Ain spoke up in code, Faid had to translate, "Shion has been infiltrated by armed Atlantea Federation troops. They are located in the heart of the city and have taken over the adjoining mining areas."

"Have the kedek mining levels to the asklodite been interrupted?" asked Gloughster. He knew the answer to the question already he just wanted to hear what Isk was going to say.

"We have not had any news from the mining organization since a month ago," said the minister.

"What does the Atlantea Federation have to say about that?" asked Lino after picking up a prompt from Gloughster.

Isk hesitated, "we are not aware of any mining rights."

Gloughster got angry and put his hands on the table and stood up. "The Atlantea Federation will remove itself from Shion!"

Isk began to speak in Jannai and slowly stood up. Gloughster answered him back. The two of them raised their voices. They went at each other. Gailen had a headset on. The Captain came over the communication line and said that there were some changes in the deployment of the ships from the Atlantea Federation. Isk sparked up his aegis. The whole room saw that. Lino followed the conversation subconsciously because he was psychic but they were really going at it. They were talking about other locations and strategy.

Gloughster raised his voice and spoke in the international language, "I will blow them off the face of the planet!" The minister had a pained look on his face.

Isk began to speak in Jannai again. He put his aegis out, sat down and crossed his arms.

"Pull them out!" shouted Gloughster. Isk closed his eyes and sent to someone.

"They are pulling out," said Isk.

Ain waved off screen and then someone came into view. They whispered to each other and then Ain spoke in code and Faid translated. "The Atlantea Federation has given word they are pulling out of the mines. The troops are preparing to leave. The Packrats will ensure the mining quotas will be restored."

"So the Atlantea Federation came into Shion for the mining rights?" asked Gloughster. He was going to make Isk answer in front of all the people assembled. Isk hesitated. He knew that Gloughster was baiting him. Isk stood up to leave.

"Shion is of no use to us for anything other than the ore. They are a worthless pacifist country. They don't even have a military. We have what information we came for. Jaiz' servant gave us everything we needed. Kill him. He is of no use any longer. You already sacrificed Jaiz. Your country does not hold a monopoly on righteousness. You are no better than us."

"We do not kill indiscriminately," said Gloughster. He was angry. Isk was playing with him. Gloughster may have been a Trance Channeler but he was new to politics at this level. Isk had been doing this for longer than him. Gloughster had already lost his cool in front of Isk. That would have to be reprimanded.

Isk turned around and took a step back into the room, "oh, now are you sure that is true? I believe you blew up one of your unarmed vessels that had wandered somewhere it should not have been. You didn't even rescue them. You tell me you don't kill indiscriminately?"

Isk walked out and passed Sati in the hall. He tapped him and discovered he was partially Jannai. The guards at the door accompanied Isk. Gloughster closed out the meeting and turned off the heads up display.

"That was very unprofessional," said Gailen. Gloughster gathered up the papers on the table.

"You did not need to give in to emotion like that," said Lino. "We will let Shion into the union but it will take some time until they are ready to come into the fold. I want that country stable before we allow them access."

"He baited me," said Gloughster.

Gailen pulled Gloughster aside and gave him a lecture. Lino went back to his cabin. He took off his uniform and put on a t-shirt and jeans. He was off for the next few hours. He went to the closet to pull something out, but someone grabbed him from behind and starked choking him.

"Little prince" came the familiar voice. It was Isk. Lino struggled under Isk's hold. He kicked him but Isk would not let him go. Isk threw him down on the floor and then released his nails. Isk froze Lino in place. Isk was in a new body. This one was not a warrior.

"I should kill you," said Isk.

"Something is wrong," said Gloughster interrupting Gailen. He psi located Lino and ran down the hall.

"If I kill the Emperor, you lose," said Isk picking up Lino by the collar. He ran his nails across Lino's cheek and then stabbed him in the chest and held his nails inside his body releasing the poison. He waited for a long time and then extracted his nails and dropped Lino. He locked the door, put a block on it so that no one could teleport in, put a block on Lino and teleported out to the helicopter. He signaled the pilot and the helicopter on the deck took off back to the Atlantea Federation lead vessel.

Gloughster arrived at Lino's cabin with two guards and tried to teleport inside but he couldn't. He called out to Lino who did not answer. He was bleeding and the poison was starting to affect him. It was the same poison that had given him the blood infection from before.

Gloughster banged on the door. Lino sent to him. Gloughster sent a psi pusle at the door but it wouldn't move.

"I need you to open this door," Gloughster said emphatically to the guards who tried to bust it open but it would not budge. "Cut it open if you have to." One of the guards left and returned with an electric saw.

Gloughster could feel Lino's consciousness fading in the timestream. He should have seen this coming. He was not paying attention. The relentless flow of the timstream was wearing on him. He was missing things. The guard cut the lock off the door but the door still wouldn't open. Isk had blocked the room. They would have to remove the door. Gloughster sent to Raven but he was still out in the frame. There would be no one to heal Lino.

"You need to heal yourself," called Gloughster through the door.

Lino very weakly put his hand up to his chest and tried to heal himself but his aegis sparked on and off. Lino's eyes lit up but he was too weak to heal himself. The poison was ravaging his body. He dropped his hand, tried to push off the floor and move onto the bed. The guard continued cutting a hole in the door. Gloughster called out to him. Lino put his hand back on his chest to try to heal himself. Gloughster was hysterical. He could not get to him. Lino's eyes lit up but it didn't help. Isk must have done something to him when he put the block on the door.

The guard finished cutting the hole and stood up and kicked in the door. Gloughster went to Lino.

"Go get the doctor," yelled Gloughster, "and inform Gailen."

Gloughster sat down next to Lino and hugged him as Lino started to fall over. Gloughster cradled his head in his hands and brushed the hair out of his eyes. Lino kept trying to heal himself. Gloughster put his hand on Lino's chest and took a deep breath.

"Take my life force," he said and Gloughster's hand glowed on Lino's chest. Lino's aegis sparked on and his eyes lit up as he started to heal himself. The doctor came in the room.

"He has a blood infection," said Gloughster. He could see that in the timestream. The doctor came in with a medical bag. He put the plasma plastic container on the top bunk and then put the line in Lino's arm. He then took out a hyper inject syringe and some penicillin, shot him up in the arm then gave Lino a synth shot.

The All Hands message came over the intercom. Gailen came in the room.

"What happened to him?"

"Isk poisoned him. Raven is not here to heal him. He has a blood infection again, I don't know if we will be able to stop it. He is going to get really sick," said Gloughster.

"Why didn't you see this in the timestream?" asked Gailen.

"I was so busy dealing with Shion."

"You are the Emperor's life Gloughster. You need to keep it together."

"I know that. It won't happen again."

"If he dies…" trailed off Gailen.

"I know that," said Gloughster and stood up. "I know." Gloughster helped Lino onto the bed as he continued to try to heal himself.

"Stop," said Gloughster as Lino layed down. He put his hand on Lino's arm. "Stop, you are sick, you need to save your strength."

It had been a week since they had left Shion, Lino was very sick. He had lost weight and had hardly been eating. They had to increase his neurocyne injections because he needed his aegis under control so that he could keep the infection at bay with his healing power. He came into the cafeteria and sat down with Sati and Nathaneal.

"You look terrible. You look like a neurocyne addict," said Sati.

"I have a blood infection. I ran into that Jannai that ripped up my back. You remember the scars."

"What are you two talking about?" asked Nathaneal.

"You didn't hear? The Jannai that came to the Shion negotiation tried to assassinate the Emperor before he left the ship. The Trance Channeler didn't see it in the timestream," said Sati.

"I thought the Trance Channeler had to see all those kind of things?" asked Nathaneal.

"Gloughster is new to politics like this," said Lino and then started coughing. He put his hand up to his mouth and turned away.

"Are you grounded too?"

"Yes, I can't fly in this condition. I can hardly stand let alone eat something. Food makes me sick. I am going to get real skinny again like I was when I first started taking the neurocyne."

Lino started shivering as they called for him over the comm to go to the Command Center. He got up from the table very slowly.

"You need to get some rest," said Sati.

"I'll be fine. It will just take some time."

Lino didn't know that. He felt terrible. He put his hand on his stomach and it lit up as he started sending healing energy into himself. He had learned to do that when he felt like he was going to faint. He found it hard to climb the stairs and he didn't dare teleport. He might fall out on the floor. That had happened the last time he teleported. He was panting when he came into the Command Center.

"Your Majesty," said the Captain. Lino saluted weakly and leaned into the table.

Gailen handed Lino a cable. Lino put it down on the holographic map and looked at it. He needed to hold on to the table to ensure he didn't fall down. He was dizzy.

"Good, Anis has accepted Shion into the Pacific Territories. Now we don't have to worry about that any more. Where is the Atlantea Federation fleet and have we joined the Esset yet?" asked Lino, he started to sway a little bit and held onto the table tighter. Gailen could see he was unsteady.

An officer handed Lino the binoculars. Lino didn't take them. He couldn't look through them right now. He would have to remove his hands from the table.

"Are you alright?" asked Gailen. He could see Lino holding onto the table tightly.

"I feel kind of sick," said Lino. "I think I need to go."

Gloughster came into the Command Center and walked over to the radar officer and started talking to him. The radar officer confirmed something for him. Gloughster turned around to the Captain, "the Atlantea Federation is going to attack us."

"What have you seen Gloughster?"

"You need to scramble the frames. They are going to target us specifically because the Emperor is here."

The Captain turned to Lino.

"I authorize whatever he says," said Lino and started coughing uncontrollably. He leaned over and put his hand on his stomach. It hurt. Lino stopped coughing and turned to walk out of the Command Center. He started to sway and then collapsed.

"Lino," called out Gloughster. Gailen leaned down to him and helped him up. Lino was sweating and had a fever.

"I will take him to the infirmary," said Gailen helping him out of the Command Center and down the stairs. Gailen sent to Raven to meet them in the infirmary. The doctor put Lino on fluids and scanned him with the handheld.

"His immune response is virtually non-existent," said the doctor as he gave Lino a synth shot. "There is not much more I can do for him but to make him comfortable, he needs to be healed."

Raven came in the infirmary and saw Lino on the table. He was conscious but had a hard time keeping his eyes open.

"Is it the same thing as before?" asked Raven.

"I need you to get through the block this time," said Gailen.

"I don't know if I can do that," said Raven.

"You still have the augmenter, right?"

"Yes, there will be no issue raising my level but if he is that sick it may actually harm him more if I try to take the block down."

"We need to try this," said Gailen.

"This is going to hurt him," Raven stated.

Gailen sent to Gloughster and asked if Lino was going to die. Gloughster sent back that was not what he saw in the timestream.

"Lino, this may hurt," said Raven as he lifted up Lino's shirt and placed his hands on his stomach. Lino was only half conscious. He did not register what Raven was saying. Raven sent healing energy into him. It took some time for Raven to start the healing because he had to determine what his status was first.

Raven put the augmenter on his wrist and then replaced his hands on Lino's stomach. He felt the infection. It had completely overtaken Lino's system. Lino was very sick. His ability to heal himself was the only thing keeping him stable.

"I have to do this rapidly or it is not going to make a difference," said Raven.

Lino started to hallucinate his fever was high. Raven put his hands over Lino's eyes and told him to close his eyes that this would hurt. Raven boosted his power using the augmenter and his level raised to 80 quickly. He focused a surge of healing energy into Lino and his body went rigid. It was painful. Lino started to scream.

"He is fighting it," said Raven. Even though Raven was healing him, the block that Isk had put on Lino this time made it so that his body did not want to heal. His own cells were fighting to infect him. Raven latched on to the nanomachines and then sent to Faid and asked him to bring the handheld. Faid materialized to his signal.

"You need to activate the Right to Survive program for him," said Raven. "I don't know how long I can fight this off for him."

Faid tapped the side of Lino's jack and plugged the terminus into the handheld and punched up the commands to the Right to Survive program that would influence Lino's Nanomachines to heal him. Raven would continue to heal him as the nanomachines did their work but it would be better if they let the nanomachines handle the majority of the repair. The handheld seemed to come to life with activity. The nanomachines were sending data back to the machine and it was not a good outcome.

"Isk affected the nanomachines?" asked Faid. He showed the handheld to Gailen. It read a critical error message.

"I don't know what that means," said Gailen.

"It means the nanomachines can't heal him, " said Faid.

"How did Isk do that?" asked Raven.

"He must have put a block on him. That is the only way that it would stop the nanomachines. We would have to unjack him, but the way that Riuho put that jack in him, there is no way that can be removed. You have to heal him with your power," said Faid tapping the side of Lino's head to retract the terminus cable.

Raven closed his eyes and boosted his power again. The augmenter read 100. His hands glowed white hot and they were warm. Raven's eyes started to glow and his aegis began to spark around his body.

Don't go psi crit now," said Faid.

"You may have to actually stop me if that happens," said Raven who took control of Lino's cells and had them attack the infection. Lino was out cold. When Raven had boosted his power it had been too much for Lino to remain conscious. Raven had knocked him out. It would make it easier to heal him and there would be no resistance. Lino's aegis started to spark in reaction to the healing energy that Raven was sending into him.

"Be careful, that is an implosion waiting to happen," said Faid. Gailen backed up.

Raven's aegis continued to spark and grew out into an energy sphere. His eyes were still glowing. Lino woke up on the table and grabbed Raven by the arm.

"Stop, you are hurting yourself," said Lino.

Raven was panting. He took his hands off Lino and his eyes stopped glowing.

"That is dangerous for you to use your power to that level," said Lino.

"We had to heal the Emperor," said Raven. "It is my duty."

Lino put his hand back on his stomach and sat up. He sent healing energy into himself. The doctor came back over and he put the handheld up to him and read his immune response. It was within the normal range now but he was still reading an infection.

"Do you feel any better?" asked the doctor.

"I feel better, like I can heal myself again," said Lino.

"We will keep you on the penicillin. This infection is harsh to your organs. I don't want you to go into renal failure. It is imperative that you drink a lot of fluids and focus on that if you need to heal yourself."

"I will remember," said Lino and got up off the table. He was a little shaky.

"Be gentle," said the doctor.

"You need to rest," said Raven.

"I am alright now," said Lino and went to leave. He was very tired. He went back to his room and laid down. Gloughster knocked on the door and came in the room closing the door behind him. He sat down next to Lino and pushed the hair out of his eyes. Lino had just cut his hair because it was annoying him. He had bangs now and hair that hung longer on the sides than in the back. It kind of made him look like a punk. His hair had grown out since it had been blonde so it was two different colours.

"How do you feel?" asked Glouyghster.

"I feel like crap, and I am cold," said Lino.

"You are going to get very sick again relatively soon. What I have seen in the timestream scares me."

Lino had been throwing up in the bathroom. He had lost more weight and had tried to eat something and it had not agreed with him. He was starving but he just couldn't eat anything. He wiped his mouth on some tissue paper and threw the paper in the trash walking back to his room holding his stomach. Gloughster was there. He had been waiting for him.

"You need to lay down," said Gloughster.

"No, the room spins it is better if I stand," said Lino.

"At least sit down."

"What is happening?" asked Lino.

Gloughster looked away from him. That is how he acted if he didn't want to lie. Gloughster looked up at the clock on the wall.

"Sit down Lino."

"Why?" Lino coughed out and then started coughing uncontrollably.

"You need to throw up or you are going to die," said Gloughster.

Lino would not stop coughing. His whole body hurt. Isk had put a time limit on the block he had put on him. Lino leaned over and tried to stick his fingers down his throat. It felt like there was something moving inside his stomach.

"Hurry up or I will need to take control of you," said Gloughster.

Lino kept coughing and gagged and almost threw up. He was leaned over. It felt terrible.

"Try harder," said Gloughster, his voice was emphatic. He was scared.

Lino threw up explosively and the black liquid was chunky.

"What is that?" asked Lino disgusted. He had to throw up again. He put his fingers back down his throat and more black liquid came out. He was sweating and his aegis had started to spark as his eyes were glowing. He leaned over and threw up for a long time. It just kept coming up. Lino fell to his knees. Gloughster leaned down and put his hand on Lino's stomach. Gloughster's hand lit up.

"Okay, that's better, but now you have to contend with…"

Isk had more than poisoned Lino he had put something inside of him. Lino put his hand on his stomach and tried to heal himself. Gloughster also leaned in and infused part of his life force. Lino opened his mouth and something that looked like a slug dropped out of his mouth and crawled on the floor. It had traveled up his esophagus from his stomach. He scrambled away from it and backed into the closet.

"What is that?" Lino asked pointing, "that was inside of me?"

"It is a kedek parasite. They live in the kedek pools. That is why it has been hard for you to keep your aegis active. It was feeding off your codess. They usually do not get that large but your codess level is high."

"How did Isk do that?" Lino trailed off. He didn't want to know.

"That was what was killing you. Isk timed the poison. If I had not seen this in the timestream it would have continued feeding off you and you could have died."

Lino put his hand on his stomach and stood up and then leaned over and puked again. Gloughster stomped on the parasite and ground it into the floor. Lino stuck out his tongue and continued to gag. Gloughster took the handheld he had with him and scanned Lino. His immune response was normal but he still had the infection.

"You should be able to heal yourself better now and you should feel like you have more energy."

"I actually feel better now. Isk really does not like me."

"Isk has a job to do, like I have a job to do. But I need to be better prepared. It should not have taken me this long to get this to you. We should have been here sooner and you would not have had to go through as rough a time.

"Gloughster stop beating yourself up, you are new at this."

"No, the Trance Channeler needs to be ahead of these things. I am screwing up."

"Gloughster please, wait a moment. We all have a lot to learn here. This is new to all of us. You cannot take the burden of all this on your own. You need to let people help you."

Gloughster started to get very angry. His eyes began to glow. He took a swipe at Lino and advanced on him. Gloughster picked up Lino by the collar and raised him off the ground. His voice was low and had a malignant undertone to it laced with sending, the same as Justine had when she got angry with him.

"I am a Trance Channeler, you are my Emperor. You need to discipline what you own."

Gloughster dropped Lino and stormed out of the room. Lino had never seen Gloughster act like that. It was against his nature. The evolution had really changed him. Gloughster left the door open when he left and Saya came to the door.

"Gloughster said you needed something cleaned up?" asked Saya.

"Don't let him treat you like a slave Saya. I can clean up my mess."

"No, your Majesty. It is my duty as the Adept to look after you and Gloughster," she said. "Did you get very sick?"

"You knew this was going to happen Saya?"

"Gloughster told me this days ago your Majesty. He tells me everything these days. I think it helps him to deal with the relentless pull of the timestream."

"He didn't tell me until it happened."

"He was not supposed to tell you at all. He was really worried. He broke a tenet of the timestream by telling you. He loved you too much your Majesty to let you suffer."

"Why what will happen to him," Lino was concerned for him now.

"The nightmares and hallucinations will start again."

"Again Saya? What is going on?" He took Saya's arm and made her stop cleaning the floor. She looked up at him.

"Gloughster has been beating himself at night to try to keep the timestream at bay. Raven has been healing him every morning."

Lino released her and teleported to Gloughster's signal. He was in the cabin he had been in before. He had his Trance Channeler jumpsuit down at his waist and was beating his back with the end of a belt. The buckle was leaving marks on his skin. He was startled as Lino grabbed his hand and made him stop. Lino put his hand on Gloughster's back. He could see the welts from the belt buckle. There was a juice syringe laying next to the bed. Gloughster pulled his arms away from Lino and took the belt in both hands.

"I am screwing up. I have to be punished and you have not done it, so someone had to."

"I will not have my Trance Channeler flagellating himself."

"I have to," said Gloughster and went to the closet and pulled out a book and handed it to Lino.

"What is this?" Lino turned it over and opened the cover.

"It is the religious tenets for Trance Channelers. The Prophets in the Jannassee Islands gave it to me when I became the Emperor's Trance Channeler.

"You went to the Jannassee Islands?"

"I went to kill your father."

"What? Gloughster, you killed my father!"

"I slit your father's throat in his sleep and then I killed Justine."

"How could you do that?"

"The evolution has made me into a monster."

"You evolved before the Emperor was assassinated?"

"Yes Lino," said Gloughster matter of factly. "There has been a plot to kill your father ever since he became the Emperor. You were in danger as well. The person that tried to assassinate you was sent by your father."

"My own father tried to have me killed?"

"Yes, that affront had to be remedied. That was unacceptable."

"How do you have the strength to kill people?"

"Your father is not the only person I killed Lino."

"What are you saying Gloughster?"

"I killed all his head ministers. I am a monster."

Lino took a step back from him and put up his hands. Gloughster took the belt and handed it to Lino who took the belt and then Gloughster picked up the book from the bed and opened it. He shuffled the pages and then handed the book to Lino who read the passage.

"100 lashings for a single infraction? Gloughster, this is cruel. But you save me. You told me about the parasite."

"That is an infraction Lino, I was not supposed to tell you. You were supposed to get sicker and almost die. I did not do what the timestream instructed me to."

"Who told you to follow these tenets?" Lino asked and kept reading. It was barbaric some of the things it was asking. "You are supposed to fast three days a week?"

"Yes Lino, but I have not been able to keep to that. I am ashamed."

"And you are supposed to take juice?"

"It heightens the connection to the timestream but I have not been keeping up with it. It is too much. You should punish me for not meeting up to my responsibilities." Gloughster took the book out of Lino's hands and pushed the belt into his chest.

"Do it Lino."

Gloughster turned his back to Lino and put his hands up to his face. Lino did not want to do this. He backed up from Gloughster and took the belt in his hand by the buckle and started to hit him with it.

"Do it harder," said Gloughster.

Lino stood behind Gloughster and kept hitting him with the belt. Gloughster put his hands up on the top bunk to brace himself from the hits. He seemed to be sending feelings of relief and not pain from being hit. Lino didn't understand why. The pain actually felt good it kept the timestream at bay and kept Gloughster's mind clear. It had been wearing on him the constant pulling of the timestream and he had been starting to hallucinate regularly. He was losing touch with what was reality and what was the timestream. Lino stopped hitting him.

"There, I will not hit you any more," said Lino and threw the belt down on the bottom bunk.

Gloughster wiped his eyes before he turned around and pulled up his jumpsuit and put his arms in the sleeves zipping it up.

"Thank you."

"Why didn't you tell me that this was happening? That you were having nightmares and hallucinating."

"You have the blood infection to deal with. It is not my place to bother you with such things."

"But you can request to have me beat you? What is going on Gloughster these rules are crazy, how can you live up to this?"

Gloughster took the juice syringe and put it at his palm. "It is my duty. It is tradition. I need to embrace it and I am not. I am scared Lino."

"What are you scared of?"

"That I will lose myself in the evolution," Gloughster threw the syringe on the bed and turned away from Lino putting his hand on the top bunk and leaning in. "I will become ruthless. I don't like the way it feels Lino. It makes me crazy."

"You need to handle your responsibility, like I have to handle mine. It is not like I have a choice either. Maybe if you had embraced it you would not have been all emotional with Isk. That was a bad showing for us with Shion.

"I know," said Gloughster. "I need to be alone now." Gloughster turned away from Lino who leaned in and hugged him before he left. He knew this was hard for Gloughster, but he had faith in him.

Lino had been cleared to fly. He still had the blood infection but he was feeling better. The Escalon had joined the Esset battlefleet again. They were on their way to the Atlantea Federation homeland to wage a full-scale assault on their Londes base. Lino climbed into the frame and initiated the start up sequence and jacked in. He flicked the switches over his head and checked the pin drive. The heads up display came up and the front windows of the cockpit lit up so that he could see across the hangar. He pushed the start up buttons and brought the frame to a static hover. Lino moved the frame forward and set it down on the catapult clamps beneath the launch tube. The frame docked with the clamps and then moved up into the catapult launch tube. The lights along the floor of the tube were lit up and were flashing. They would turn solid when the catapult was in the ready position. The launch placard came down with the word 'Abort' on it, at all the stages and a red light panel. Lino checked the seat harnass and anchored his feet on the pedals. The sword modules were loaded onto the side of the legs and the gennen rifle was attached to the back of the frame. The wings were folded down at the back of the frame, flush with the body. He would reconfigure on launch. The catapult made a loud sound and Lino knew it was set. The placard lit up 'Launch' and the lights turned green. He gave acknowledgement.

"Lino Dejarre. Isshin F22-15 launching!"

The catapult sent the frame down the tube and then thrust it into the air. Lino gave it some time to clear the Escalon. The transform command could be initiated with his psi. It was faster if he just let his psi and the jack handle it. His Isshin was set up like his other frame had been with the all around psi synch but he didn't really need to use it with the jack. It was just an extra setting in the case the jack connection was lost. Lino transformed to aircraft mode.

Lino was up with Sati and Nathaneal. Lino on Sati's left side.

"You are supposed to be off my right wing," said Sati.

"No, I want to be on this side so I can see you before you go off half cocked after the Streak."

"He does tend to bank right," said Nathaneal over the comm. Nathaneal was the lead.

"He's out here I can feel it," said Sati.

"What, you can feel him now?" asked Lino.

"Sati has this thing. He says he can feel the Streak's codess energy when he is up. I think he is full of crap," said Nathaneal.

"No, I can feel him," said Sati. "He's up here now and he is close."

"What are you three having a tea party? Cut the chatter," came the communications officer in the Command Center.

"One bogey at 10 miles, 5 o'clock closure."

"They are out pretty far," said Gailen.

"Nathaneal, is he a single?" asked Sati.

Nathaneal went up into the clouds and disappeared. Lino stayed off Sati's left. One blip changed into two on Nathaneal's radar screen.

"He has a friend. Wait, no there are three," said Nathaneal as he looked at his screen.

"Permission to engage?" came Sati.

Lino could see that Sati was itching to go. Lino moved his frame a little further away from Sati just in case he went off crazy in either direction. The bogeys came past them and then banked and turned after them.

"They are coming around," said Nathaneal coming back into view. Sati started to move off from Lino. One of the frames was white. Sati felt something familiar. He sent out his psi and the codess feeling was the same.

"That is the Streak!" said Sati. Lino slowed down. He wanted to be far away from Sati when he ran off after the Streak. Someone locked on to Lino and fired the guns. Lino veered off and banked. His pursuer transformed and took out the sword module. Lino transformed along with him and went to attack the frame. Nathaneal came out of the clouds, transformed and went after another frame with the gennen rifle. Sati blew past them the Streak following him.

The Streak was pushing Sati forward. He was on him directly. Sati turned off the limiter and climbed. The Streak followed right behind him. Lino struck his pursuer and blew up the frame. Lino came around. Nathaneal fired on the frame and hit it in the cockpit and it burst into flames and fell out of the sky. Sati was on his own. Nathaneal went to help him and Lino followed.

Sati teleported the frame but the Streak seemed to be able to predict his moves. Sati could not shake him. He came over land. An arial warning came over Sati's instruments and a message came on the screen. He was too close to the beacon and the No-Fly Zone area.

"You are out too far. Do not go into No-Fly Zone," came the Command Center over the comm.

A voice came over Sati's comm line. "Unidentified aircraft you are currently flying over Atlantea Federation No-Fly Zone 15 disengage immediately."

"This is Isshin F22-12 requesting permission to fly through airspace."

"Isshin F22-12 permission denied. This is Atlantea Federation No-Fly Zone 15 disengage."

Guns started firing from the ground.

"Crap!" said Sati and banked. He came around.

Aircraft were scrambled from the ground.

"They are too close, F22-12 has already penetrated zone," said the radar officer from the Escalon.

Nathaneal and Lino were called back.

"I can't leave him out there," said Nathaneal.

"You can't fly in there either. He is on his own," said Lino.

Nathaneal and Lino went back to the ship. Sati disarmed and was escorted with missiles locked on out of the No-Fly Zone.

Gloughster was in the Command Center on the comm. He was negotiating with the Command Center in the No-Fly Zone trying to ensure that there were no diplomatic implications to Sati's little visit. Gloughster was being very direct and the comm officer that was listening to him was a little shocked at his demeanor.

The minute that Sati was out of the No-Fly Zone the Streak was on him again. The Streak had been waiting for him. He went after him full on aggressive and fired a missile. Sati was recalled but he couldn't disengage. The Streak followed him back in.

"Get that frame out of here!" said the Captain. "Shoot him down."

Sati came and the guns went off while he was in range firing at the Streak as it crossed into the airspace surrounding the Escalon. Sati blew past the Escalon. The Streak teleported and withdrew.

Sati was escorted up to the Command Center when he landed. Sati was holding his helmet as the guard brought him into the Command Center.

Gloughster walked up to him. "Sati Ima!" ground out Gloughster. He said it low and it was laced with sending.

"Yes, your Eminence," said Sati. He could not resist Gloughster's psychic influence.

"We are at war. You do not do as you like. You were warned to stay out of the No-Fly Zone."

"I was being pursued by a hostile."

"You were not supposed to fly into the No-Fly Zone."

Sati opened his mouth.

"Do not speak!" yelled Gloughster. "You are grounded indefinitely. You could have started an incident in Shalany." Gloughster was furious.

The guard put his hand on Sati's arm and escorted him out.

Lino passed Sati on the way down the stairs from the Command Center.

"I'm grounded," said Sati as the guard pushed him forward. "Your Trance Channeler is mean."

Lino came into the Command Center. Gloughster was still on the comm with the Shalany Command Center. He was being very politically correct. He finally disconnected.

"So did we stop an international incident?" asked Lino.

"For now," said Gloughster. He was still angry. Lino was picking up pain from the tap he had on him. Gloughster vanished. Lino stayed in the Command Center for a while and asked about the Esset. The Captain gave him some information and then dismissed him.

Lino went to the cafeteria before he went back to his room. Nathaneal was leaving as Lino came in. Nathaneal walked out of the cafeteria and went back to his room. Sati was in there holding his hyper inject syringe at his wrist.

"What are you doing?" asked Nathaneal coming in and closing the door.

"I got grounded," said Sati holding up the syringe.

"And what are you doing with my red?"

"Racing thoughts. The Streak is coming," said Sati.

"Don't Sati. You don't need it. Go to the doctor instead."

"No, I need to feel something," Sati rolled up his sleeve and put the syringe at his arm.

Nathaneal moved in to pull the syringe away from Sati's arm but Sati was too fast and shot himself up. It took a moment but his eyes started to glow. Red was very volatile with Sati. The drug could make him very angry or make him go crazy. Nathaneal was never comfortable with Sati on red. Sati's head began to fall forward and he leaned over sitting on the bottom bunk. He started to nod but tried to keep himself from falling on the floor. He put his hand out to steady himself. Sati almost fell on the floor but stopped himself and looked up at Nathaneal. Sati's eyes were glowing. Sati stood up and took a step forward.

"Sati?" said Nathaneal and put his hands up. Sati started to growl. He put his hands out and down and his nails started to grow. The nails came out to sharp points. Sati lowered his head and looked up at Nathaneal. He opened his mouth and started to drool.

"Sati back off." Nathaneal took a step back and backed into the desk. Sati advanced on him and raised his hands. Sati ran at Nathaneal and attacked him.

Lino got some soup but didn't really eat it. Blue came to sit with him. The doctor had removed the bandage over his eye but he now had a scar that went from above his eye, over the lid and below.

"I haven't seen you in a while," said Blue.

"How is your eye?" asked Lino.

"It doesn't really hurt anymore but I am more sensitive to bright light."

"Where is Faid?"

"He is taking his test."

"Oh yes, I forgot about that," said Lino who started picking up pain again from Gloughster. He got up and dismissed himself, leavin the cafeteria. Lino went to Gloughster's room. He could hear a commotion inside. Lino tried to teleport in but there was a block on the door. There was a crashing sound and then yelling.

"I can't do that," came Gloughster's voice lound. He was talking to himself.

"Gloughster?" called out Lino.

"Go away your Majesty," Gloughster called through the door.

Something crashed on the floor. Lino closed his eyes. He was more powerful than Gloughster. Lino teleported through the block Gloughster had put on the door. There were papers and maps all over the floor and the desk was on its side. Gloughster threw a book across the room. There were four hyper inject syringes on the floor and all of them were empty. Someone knocked on the door. Lino called to them and sent them away. Lino moved into Gloughster and grabbed his arms and held them down at his sides. Gloughster gritted his teeth and struggled with Lino.

"Get off me!" Gloughster sparked up his aegis and pushed Lino back.

"Trance Channeler, what is the problem?"

"The timestream, it is relentless. I cannot keep up with it."

"Take a break Gloughster. Just stop for a moment."

"No, your Majesty it is coming and you are not ready. And we have to get them."

"Get whom Gloughster?"

"We have to blow them off the map because of Sati I have to sacrifice all those people."

"What do you mean?"

"Shinlan is next to Shalany. They are going to attack them. They just needed an excuse. Sati gave them that excuse. We have to sacrifice the Shinlan territory and let them attack. Then we need to retaliate and I need to blow them off the map. I don't want to do that."

"Then don't Gloughster."

"I have no choice. It is in the timestream."

"You told me when I was sick."

"That is different. You were just going to get sicker."

"What do you mean I am not ready?"

"The Convergence your majesty," said Gloughster defeated. "All of the outcomes are the same. I have researched them all. I have even tried to change the timestream. I am not powerful enough to do that. I don't want to evolve again. I will lose myself and I can't do that. I can't kill Saya she has to bear your child. I am trapped.

"What are you talking about Gloughster?"

"You are going to die in the Convergence. Nothing I can do will stop that."

"You told me you had seen alternate outcomes before?"

"Only once. Of all the outcomes I have seen I have only seen that one once. I have not seen it again. You are not ready."

"When is the Convergence?"

"You are not ready."

"But we are not near the palace in the City. I am going to miss it."

"No Lino, the Convergence happens to a person. It will happen wherever you are. When you were at the Psi Faction and in the palace that is what I saw. You are here. It will happen here."

"On the ship?"

"Yes, your Majesty. Everyone will be in danger on this vessel during the Convergence."

"Then the Escalon needs to move away from the fleet."

"No, your Majesty. With the unsteady situation in Shalany we cannot afford to move away from the fleet. Shalany has to be sacrificed along with Shinlan, otherwise it will escalate the war and we cannot have that.

"I cannot endanger all these people Gloughster. You have to get me off this ship."

"I tried that, your Majesty. We were going to take you to Shalany but Sati screwed that up with his little trip into the No-Fly Zone."

"Try again Gloughster."

All of a sudden Lino's hair started to stand up on his head and he felt power surging through him.

The weather officer in the Command Center made a comment on the rapidly changing weather pattern.

"There is a funnel system that looks like it is forming," he said.

"On the water?" asked the Captain.

"Yes, that is what it looks like. The weather pattern is crazy," said the weather officer.

Lino started to raise up off the floor in the cabin and his aegis began sparking.

"Put your arms out to the side and do not touch the wall," said Gloughster.

"Why?" asked Lino moving away from the wall.

"You need to ground yourself. Take off any metal you have on."

Lino pulled off his shirt and his belt and droppedf them on the floor. He had the metal bars and his wings on his shirt. Lino's eyes started to light up.

"What is happening Gloughster?"

"The Convergence is coming."

"Why didn't you warn me?"

"The Convergence was not due for months. Something has changed the timestream."

An alarm went off inside the ship.

"We have a massive energy surge on the fifth level in the living quarters," said an officer. Another officer confirmed the reading.

"Where is it?" asked Gailen.

"It seems to be coming from the Trance Channeler's quarters."

"Where is the Emperor?" asked Gailen.

"I don't know why do you ask?"

"He is the Converger."

"What? Are you telling me that the Emperor is the Converger and that this could happen here?" asked the Captain. "This vessel is in danger. Gailen, why didn't you warn us?

"We did not think the Convergence was due for months. The tour would be up by then and we would have taken them back to the Psi Faction. There was no reason to bore you with those details."

"He is the Emperor and the Converger. We cannot have him flying any longer. He is too valuable to the Pacific Territories."

"He will overrule you sir," said Gailen. "His Trance Channeler will never ground him. Their relationship is too close."

"He will have no choice. I am the Captain and I say he does not fly anymore."

"You cannot authorize that. You have to take it up with Izen," said Gailen.

"Lightening sir," said the weather officer.

Huge lightening strikes started to converge around the Escalon. Lino could feel the lightening. His aegis started to spark out of control around him. There was a knock on the door. The Captain had sent some guards to Gloughster's cabin. Gloughster opened the door. They could see Lino hovering off the floor with his arms out.

"Do not come in here. It is dangerous," said Gloughster motioning the guards back.

Lino's aegis was sparking out around him and the lightening was hitting the ship. Lino's hair was standing up and sparks of lightening were shooting out of his hands. His eyes started to light up and then the lightening hit the ship and funneled through the metal and came out of the wall and went through Lino. The lightning came shooting out of his hands and circled around the room. Gloughster backed up into the hall and motioned anyone in the hall back. He was concerned for Lino who was not 100% healthy either. He still had the blood infection. This was going to take a lot out of him. The lightening continued to hit the ship in one steady stream.

"The surge is getting larger Captain," said the officer. They were monitoring it on their instruments. Lino's wings flew out of his back and he started to change. Gloughster saw that and closed the door staying out in the hall. He did not want anyone to see. A second blast of lightening hit the first one from outside the ship and channeled through the same conduit and hit Lino. His body jerked and then he raised his arms and the lightening shot out of his hands hitting the wall and scorching it. Then just as quickly it disappeared and the lightning stopped with the weather pattern going back to normal. Lino fell out on the floor and called to Gloughster who opened the door and walked in, closing the door behind him. Lino retracted his wings and the aegis started to die down.

"What was that?" asked Lino as Gloughster helped him up.

"The Convergence is coming. It is feeling you out."

"You talk about it as if it were alive."

"Technically Lino, it is a living conduit of kedek energy."

Chapter 10

Gloughster grounded Lino. Now that the Convergence energy had found him he did not want him up in the air in a frame that could be blown out of the sky or hit by lightening. Gloughster gave Sati back his flight privileges. Fred could not afford to have another pilot grounded now that he had lost Lino and 80% of their pilots from before.

Faid had passed his test but just barely. Blue was with him in their quarters. Blue had his hand up to his eye. It was hurting.

"Does it hurt?" asked Faid. He had been really quiet for the past few minutes. Faid was distracted. He was sensing something and he couldn't figure it out.

Blue didn't say anything. He was distracted as well.

"Something is wrong with Lino," said Blue finally.

"Yes, I am feeling something," said Faid.

Faid sent to Lino but he didn't get an answer. He tried to psi locate him but he couldn't find him. Gloughster had put up a block on him. Lino was in Gloughster's quarters, his aegis was sparking and he couldn't get it to stop.

"Have you taken your maintenance shot for the day?"

"Yes, I took more than normal because it started earlier. Do you think it is the Convergence again?" asked Lino.

"It could be but I am not sure," said Gloughster. He closed his eyes and looked into the timestream. He opened his eyes and they glowed red. Lino had never seen Gloughster actually link directly to the timestream. His whole demeanor changed, his aura had a low keen to it, and then Lino felt something frightening. This was energy that felt like death. Lino backed up from Gloughster. The timestream was swirling before his eyes, he could see the past, the present and the future all at once. He was looking at the Convergence.

Someone had changed the timestream. It felt like Isk from what Gloughster could tell but this presence was malignant. Gloughster tried to latch on to it but the minute that he did something grabbed onto his psyche and started pulling at him. Gloughster tried to pull away from the force but couldn't. He sent a psi surge at the force and was able to remove himself from it. He leaned back and snapped out of it. Lino had seen him physically move back and asked him what happened.

"There is someone manipulating the timestream. I can't tell who it is but they are very powerful. There may be another Converger."

"What do you mean another Converger? I thought there could be only one," asked Lino.

"Yes, you are correct. There can be only one Converger but they can try to groom another one and see if the energy will take with that person instead. They would need to get the level higher. I don't think we have a problem with that. Your level is very high now and the Convergence has already caught you in its wake once. I don't think we have to worry about another Converger usurping the power."

"What about me not being ready? When is the Convergence going to happen?"

"I don't know. I have not been able to see the exact day and time but it seems to be a lot sooner than it was before. It could be in the next week. It could be tomorrow. It is unclear in the timestream."

"What about Raven? You had said once before that you saw him at the Convergence."

"Yes, I saw you try to rescue him from the energy and then you were killed. That was just one of the outcomes with your death that I saw."

"Raven is here but I have not seen him for a while."

"I know that. I have separated him. His cabin has been moved. I don't want you near him for now."

"What if I need to be healed?"

"Your blood infection is better and the timestream does not show that as a liability any longer."

Gloughster put his hand up. Another Trance Channeler was communicating with him. This person was timing to him.

The Convergence is upon you. Where is the Converger? came the sending.

The Converger is near, sent Gloughster.

He is around you? sent the stranger.

**What is your designation?* sent Gloughster.

We are Jains.

You are from the Atlantea Federation?

We affiliate with no one.

How can that be the case?

We are neutral.

You are Eleni? asked Gloughster.

Yes, we are Eleni. We are neutral. The Converger is in danger.

Lino picked up a sending from Isk and then suddenly was down on the floor choking. He put his hands up to his throat. Gloughster moved over to him and put up a block around him.

Maintain the block on the Converger or he will be compromised, sent Jains.

Who is after him? sent Gloughster.

The Isk, it is Jehnen. Take control of your designation or you will lose the Convergence. You need to evolve. Kill the handmaiden and take the evolution. The Emperor does not need an heir.

I do not want to do that, sent back Gloughster.

Then you will lose the Convergence to the Atlantea Federation.

What do you mean lose the Convergence?

Jehnen has control of the timestream. You cannot fight him as an 'I' designation. You need to evolve, sent Jains.

"What is happening Gloughster?" asked Lino who could tell that someone was communicating.

Besides separating Raven from Lino, Gloughster had also sent Raven out earlier with a bomb that he would drop on Shinlan. Gloughster had been pained to do that. He did not want to have to sacrifice all those people but it was what was in the timestream. He was finding it hard to do his job. Raven had just dropped the bomb. Gloughster could see all the death in the timestream. It affected him. He leaned over on the bed. It was too much, all the minds dying.

You need to evolve. Take the life of the handmaiden, sent Jains.

"Why would you need to kill Saya?" asked Lino.

Gloughster sat down on the side of the bed defeated. He could not take this any longer. He put his head in his hands and listed to what Jains continued to send to him. Jains was adamant and then the sending just cut off.

"I have to evolve," was all Gloughster said and then told Lino to leave.

Chapter 11

Gloughster had to find a way to evolve but not have to kill Saya. He had consulted the timestream and there was only one way that he could figure he could take the life force without killing her. He would have to sacrifice the life of the child, but he figured that he could do this in such a way that the child could remain alive. Gloughster called Saya to his cabin and had her sit on the edge of the bed.

"This may be jarring," he said to her.

Gloughster closed his eyes and then opened them and they glowed red. He was looking into the timestream. He then opened the timestream overtop of Saya and himself as she was sitting on the bed. He brought her into the future. She looked down and could see that she was 9 months pregnant. It shocked her. Gloughster ensured that she was in the timestream and placed his hand on her stomach. He was going to take half of the baby's life force away so that he did not have to kill Saya. He was going to do it before the child was born. The child would be born degenerating. She leaned back. Gloughster pulled the life force from the child and his eyes lit up a bright red and his hair started to lighten. Gloughster's skin changed to a shiny white as he seemed to take on a glow to himself. He released her and put her back in the present. He snapped out of it and fell against the bed. The timestream closed and they went back to the present.

"Did you kill the child?" she asked.

Gloughster pushed off of the bed and stood up again and helped her up. She was shocked at the way he looked now, his irises were red and his hair was graying. He seemed to be moving slower than he had been and there was a glow about him. It felt as if the timestream was with him now. She could feel him. He felt more powerful than Justine had been.

"You have taken the second evolution. I can feel you now. You must select a 'J' designation," she said.

"The Emperor will name me," said Gloughster and sent to Lino.

The sending from Gloughster bore into Lino's brain. It felt different. It felt like the death sending that Lino had felt before. Lino sent back but something triggered his response. He didn't really know how he did it, but he timed to Gloughster. The name just came to him.

Jephastian is you designation, Lino sent.

Gloughster sent back to Lino who was in his cabin. The sending was influencing him somehow.

Where are you? Lino timed to Glougshter.

"Do not hurt him again," said Saya to Gloughster as he got up and went to the door. "You are more powerful now. You will not hurt him."

"I will try Saya but I can not guarantee that," said Gloughster and vanished going to meet Lino. He appeared in Lino's room.

"My Emperor," said Gloughster and bowed to Lino who blinked and looked at him, the colour of his skin was a little shocking and Gloughster's eyes were glowing red.

Chapter 12

Gloughster put the juice syringe to his wrist and sighed. He had already taken four syringe fulls of the drug and this would be his last. He could feel the juice affecting him. The timestream was coming closer. His eyes were glowing. He was nodding and leaning forward on the bed. Saya was in the room with him. He shot himself up and then put his hand up to the side of his head. The juice was affecting him. The timestream overtook him. He looked up at the ceiling and just stared. The timestream coalesced. All he could see was the Convergence. It was close. The past, present and future all came together at one time. He was watching Lino engulfed by the energy. He started to moan. Saya moved over to him. She was concerned.

Then Isk was standing in front of him. He was in the timestream and started to choke Gloughster who put his arms on Isk's and tried to pull him away. Saya started screaming. Gloughster picked up a sending from Jains.

Trap him in the timestream.

Isk had figured out how to be physically in the timestream and present at the same time. Gloughster could not remove Isk's hands from his neck. He would have to join him in the timestream.

What is your designation? sent Isk.

Gloughster took hold of the timestream, stepped into the stream where Isk was and removed Isk's hands from his neck stopping him. Isk was getting bolder. He figured he had changed the timestream and had tried to control Lino what was controlling the Trance Channeler.

"Jehnen!" screamed Gloughster and took control of Isk and stopped him. The timestream closed. Isk did not know Gloughster's designation except for Izen. This would be beneficial to Gloughster. If he could keep that secret he would have the upperhand.

Gloughster sat back down on the bed. He felt dizzy. Saya was concerned for him. The timestream had not overtaken him yet, but it was coming.

"How do you feel?" she asked. She was looking for something specific. He layed back on the bed and had her sit next to him. "This is hard for you."

Gloughster nodded to her. This was very difficult for him. He was not used to the constant pull of the timestream and even though he had been a Prince and was familiar with politics he could not keep up.

"I cannot deal with this Saya. It is too much."

"You are new at this Gloughster. It will take some time for you to get used to this. Just like it took Justine."

"But this is so much different that what it was. When Lino became the Emperor everything changed. I have killed people Saya and I cannot take that back." Gloughster leaned back and put his hand up to his head and closed his eyes. The room was spinning and he was beginning to hallucinate.

"Can you see yourself yet?" she asked.

"What do you mean Saya?" he said looking over at her.

"Then it hasn't started yet. You rest. The hallucination will come upon you soon. You must be ready for it."

"Hallucination, what hallucination?"

"The timestream will show you your biggest fear. You will need to be ready for it."

"Will it be about Lino?" Gloughhster turned to her and looked up at her concerned.

She leaned in to him over the bed and put her hand on his chest and told him to rest, that she would check on him later. She closed the door behind her. Saya was concerned about Gloughster. The timestream was relentless and it was cruel. Gloughster was screwing up and the timestream would not let him get away with that for very much longer. She did not have the heart to tell him that. He was being watched by the Eleni. That was the group Jains was from. The Eleni monitored the timestream and all Trance Channelers. Even though Isk was manipulating the timestream, his minder was allowing that to happen and the Eleni were standing back and watching it. But they would not let Gloughster get away with shirking his duties and not folloing the tenets of the timestream. If Isk got out of hand the Eleni would step in and try to stop him. Saya was also connected to Jains. She did not have the heart to tell Glougshter that he was on notice.

Lino had felt odd for the past day. Lino walked to the deck. He walked out into the center of the deck. He was being drawn there.

The weather officer noticed a pattern forming. He just watched it for a while and then stood up and took a pair of binoculars and looked out the front of the Command Center.

"Sir, we have a weather pattern forming. I cannot identify it."

It started to get dark out the front windows.

Lino looked out onto the deck and put his hands out to his sides and watched the sky. He was being pulled to this spot. He could see the clouds up ahead forming. They started to come racing towards the Escalon. Some of the cat officers and deck crew were pointing up at the sky. Raven was at the side of the deck, he was watching the waves. Lino didn't see him. Lino picked up a sending from Gloughster. His Trance Channler wanted to know how he was feeling.

Unexpectedly Gloughster picked up a sending from Jains.

**Beware Jephastian.*

Gloughster's eyes started to glow. Jains had taken control of him through his designation.

What would you have me do? Gloughster sent back.

The Convergence is upon you.

Gloughster tried to sit up on the side of the bed, his head hurt. He had been hallucinating. The juice had started to overtake him.

What is your command? Gloughster tried to psi locate Lino.

The sea became choppy and the clouds formed into black masses over the Escalon. The radar officer registered a large energy disturbance that was being tracked by the electrical monitor. "It is an electrical storm Captain."

The lightening started to spark in the sky. Lino's hair began to stand up on the back of his head.

"There is an energy reading on the deck," said one of the officers. Gailen took the binoculars and changed the settings to close range and looked out on the deck. He could see Lino there clearly standing in the middle of the deck. He became concerned. Raven saw Lino as well. He hadn't seen him for a while and started to walk towards him. It started to rain.

Where is your Emperor? sent Jains to Gloughster.

I do not know.

Jephasitan you are on notice.

What does that mean coming from an Eleni?

That means you will be destroyed if you do not uphold your responsibilities.

Jains sent to Gloughster and branded a double circle on his forehead. Gloughster put his hand up to his head. Saya came back in the room and asked him how he was feeling. Gloughster removed his hand from his forehead. Saya screamed his name when she saw it.

"Gloughster, you have been marked," she said.

Gloughster did not know what that meant.

"Gloughster you are in danger. You need to protect the Emperor. That is the mark of the deceased. You need to make sure you handle your responsibility or they will kill you," she was concerned. She had seen Trance Channelers marked before and they were killed quickly after the mark appeared.

You need to handle the Convergence, came Jains.

When is it? asked Gloughster.

It is happening now.

What? sent Gloughster and stood up.

"What is it?" asked Saya.

"The Convergence is happening now. Lino is in danger.

We are all in danger. Where is Raven?" He tried to psi locate Raven and found him on the deck. "What is he doing there?"

A large lightening blast hit the ship. The lights in the Command Center flickered. The lightening continued coming down on the deck. It was coming closer to Lino. The sky seemed to light up.

Gloughster got up and tried to psi locate Lino again. He couldn't locate him. Gloughster opened the timestream and could see the Convergence. He could see Lino there. It was happening now. There was no past, present and future. It was all just now.

The water started to circle around the Escalon. Lightening hit the ship directly in front of Lino and he took a step back and then suddenly he was hit by it. A stready stream of lightening came out of the clouds and the sky lit up and formed a funnel over Lino. The clouds seemed to come to the deck and circle around him. Raven couldn't see him anymore through the funnel. Raven was pushed back by the wind. Another officer came out on the deck and pushed Raven back as he tried to touch Lino's arm. The officer could not get to Lino. He was swallowed up by the cloud.

Gloughster called to Lino through the timestream but he was kicked out. His eyes lit up and he tried to get a hold of the timestream again. All he could see was the moment of Lino's death. It was happening now. The lightening let up for a moment and then a huge blast flew out of the sky. Lino anchored his feet and put one hand up to the sky with his fingers spread apart. The lightening came straight down through the funnel cloud and lit up his hand. Lino took control of it and it circled around his body and started to filter up into the cloud. The entire sky was black. All that could be seen was the lightening against the dark.

Gloughster went to the Command Center and put his hand on Gailen's shoulder.

"You are just going to leave him out there by himself?" asked Gailen.

"There is nothing that I can do for him. He has to do this on his own," said Gloughster.

"Gloughster, he is your responsibility," said Gailen.

"That may have been taken out of my hands. I have been marked," he said. Gailen could see the mark on his head and knew what that meant.

"If he dies Gloughster you will also be killed."

"Yes, I know that," said Gloughster.

Lino opened his mouth and lightening came streaming out of his hands. Lino's wings came flying out of his back and he fully changed. Raven came running and went to him. He knew Lino was trapped in the center of the funnel cloud.

"Raven..." said Gailen and handed Gloughster the binoculars.

"No, he can't be there," said Gloughster and looked through the binoculars and saw Raven. Gloughster dropped the binoculars on the holographic map table and ran out of the Command Center. He teleported to the deck.

"Raven come with me!" Gloughster screamed at him.

"Why?" said Raven fighting back the wind to move towards Lino.

"You are going to get him killed."

The lightening hit Lino again and then went off wild and almost hit Raven. Lino was trying to direct it away from the Command Center. A blast hit again and sent Gloughster and Raven down to the deck. Gloughster heard Lino scream. The lightening was burning the skin off his back and his wings were blackened from the electricity. The timestream began to circle faster around him and he could see the future in images. Gloughster sent to him. Lino whirled around. He could see Gloughster on the deck. Lino called to him.

Gloughster started to move forward but Raven held him back.

"It is not Raven who is going to get him killed, it is Gloughster," said Gailen.

Choose Trance Channeler, came the sending from Jains.

Gloughster knew what that meant. He pushed Raven back and moved towards Lino who put his hand out. Gloughster pushed through the timestream and took Lino's hand. The lightening channeled right through Lino and hit Gloughster and he was thrown across the deck. Raven ran over to him. Gloughster was burned.

Raven pulled at him and started to heal him. Lino screamed. The timestream was overtaking him. He could not hold it any longer. The lightening hit him. Lightening blasted out of his hands and hit a frame on the deck and blew it up.

Lino could feel his heart beat speeding up and it was erratic. The lightening was compromising him as he tried to channel it.

Choose the evolution Converger, came Jains.

I choose... Lino took control of the timestream and threw himself into the future. The lightening hit him and exploded.

"No!" screamed Gloughster as the funnel cloud disappeared and the lightening subsided.

Gloughster started clawing forward and ran to the spot Lino had been standing at but there was nothing. Lino was gone. The timestream started to subside. Gloughster dropped down to the deck and started to weep. He banged his hands on the deck. Raven came up to him and tried to comfort him but Gloughster pushed him away.

Gloughster just hung there silent not knowing what to do. His tears started to fall against the deck. He pounded his fist down on the metal and a wave of codess power released under his hand. He called out Lino's name quietly. Then sat back and screamed out Lino's name.

The clouds disappeared from the sky as Gloughster sat there for what seemed like hours.

Then suddenly Gloughster heard something.

"Jephastian," came a voice from above him.

Gloughster looked up and there was a figure with white wings and white skin and eyes. The figure landed in front of Gloughster gracefully and its wings unfurled out behind him. Raven put his hand up. The figure was shining like an angel. It was too bright. The angel put its hand on Glougshter's shoulder.

"Who are you?" asked Gloughster.

"I am Jin, you know me as Ameliano Dejarre," said the angel.

"How did this happen?" asked Gloughster.

(Continued in grydscaen: desecration)

Lightning Source UK Ltd.
Milton Keynes UK
UKHW010756280122
397868UK00001B/9